2.50

Praise for Laura Levine and THIS PEN FOR HIRE

"This is classic stuff: a wisecracking L.A. gal detective who solves a heinous crime and is also concerned about her thighs and personal relationship issues. I read it happily before bedtime for a week and had vivid dreams about convertibles and palm trees and blondes."

—Garrison Keillor

"Humor is the key ingredient in this slick debut . . . the story zips along to an action-filled and surprising climax. Levine delivers the goods and readers who appreciate self-deprecating humor will hope Jaine soon gets caught up in another murder."

—*Publishers Weekly*

"Laura Levine has achieved the impossible. She has written a terrific laugh-out-loud murder mystery. I would have been scared but I was too busy chuckling."

—Madelyn Pugh Davis, writer for *I Love Lucy*

"This will turn out to be a long series . . . likely to be compared to Janet Evanovich for its humor."

—*I Love a Mystery*

"Laura Levine's hilarious debut mystery, *This Pen For Hire*, is a laugh a page (or two or three) as well as a crafty puzzle. Sleuth Jaine Austen's amused take on life, love, sex and L.A. will delight readers. Sheer fun!"

—Carolyn Hart, author of the Death on Demand and Henrie O mysteries

"Jaine has a sassy attitude and I look forward to her new adventures."

—*Deadly Pleasures*

"Thank you, Laura Levine. Instead of painful crunches, I can give my abs a workout just by reading your laugh-out-loud funny book."

—Leslie Meier, author of *Father's Day Murder*

"A lot of laughs."

—*Star-News* (Pasadena)

"Laura Levine has made murder funny again! Of all the writers I've worked with, no one knows how to keep a good story zipping along like Laura. Her work is always filled not only with solid humor, but sweetness and charm."

—Mike Scully, Executive Producer of *The Simpsons*

Books by Laura Levine

THIS PEN FOR HIRE

LAST WRITES

KILLER BLONDE

SHOES TO DIE FOR

THE PMS MURDER

DEATH BY PANTYHOSE

CANDY CANE MURDER

KILLING BRIDEZILLA

KILLER CRUISE

Published by Kensington Publishing Corporation

A Jaine Austen Mystery

This Pen for Hire

Laura Levine

K

KENSINGTON BOOKS
http://www.kensingtonbooks.com

KENSINGTON BOOKS are published by

Kensington Publishing Corp.
850 Third Avenue
New York, NY 10022

All Kensington Titles, Imprints, and Distributed Lines
are available at special quantity discounts for bulk pur-
chases for sales promotions, premiums, fund-raising,
and educational or institutional use. Special book ex-
cerpts or customized printings can also be created to fit
specific needs. For details, write or phone the office of
the Kensington special sales manager: Kensington
Publishing Corp., 850 Third Avenue, New York, NY 10022,
attn: Special Sales Department, Phone: 1-800-221-2647.

First Kensington Hardcover Printing: June 2002
First Kensington Mass Market Printing: June 2003

10 9 8 7 6 5 4

Printed in the United States of America

For Mark

ACKNOWLEDGMENTS

Thanks to my agent, Evan Marshall, and my editor, John Scognamiglio, for their faith and guidance. Thanks to my husband, Mark Lacter, for cheering me every step of the way. And finally, thanks to Mr. Guy—my cat, and technical adviser—who saw to it that no cats were harmed in the writing of this novel.

Chapter One

When I wrote that letter for Howard, I hoped it would get him a date. I never dreamed it would get him arrested for murder.

I suppose I should tell you how Howard and I first met.

I'd just stepped out of the shower one unseasonably warm February day, when I heard a soft scratching at the front door, like a dog pawing to be let in. I slipped into my pink silk kimono and padded across the living room, fluffing my hair en route.

I opened the door and saw that it was not a dog, but a human being. One of my clients. A first timer. This one was a geeky guy with slicked-down hair and white socks, a veritable poster boy for pocket protectors.

He stared down at my welcome mat, clearly embarrassed.

"It's fifty dollars an hour, right?"

"That's right," I said.

"I've never done anything like this before," he mumbled.

"That's okay," I said, ushering him inside. "There's nothing to be ashamed of. Take off your jacket and relax."

No, I'm not a prostitute. I'm a writer, which in Los Angeles is often the same thing. My name is Jaine Austen (my mother is an Anglophile, and a bad speller), and I run a writing service out of my apartment called This Pen for Hire. Catchy, isn't it? I used to come up with catchy names all the time back when I worked in advertising, before I woke up one morning and decided I no longer wanted to spend the rest of my life writing stories that ended in the words "void where prohibited by law."

I write resumes. Letters. Brochures. And Personals ads. Lots of Personals ads. Maybe you've read my latest? "Rap Papa Seeks Acrobatic Mama."

I don't usually greet clients in a kimono, but Howard Murdoch was a full hour early for his appointment. He'd called me that morning, having read my ad in the Yellow Pages. He told me that he needed me to write a letter.

I left him perched on the edge of a chair in the living room while I went to change into my official work clothes: elastic-waist pants and a T-shirt.

I came out from my bedroom to find him still precariously balanced at the edge of the chair. One stiff wind and he'd be history.

"C'mon," I said, leading him into my office suite, otherwise known as my dining room.

"Have a seat," I said, gesturing to the dining table. Howard started for a chair, and I screeched in dismay.

"Hey! Don't sit on my Prozac."

I scooped my cat Prozac off the chair Howard was about to sit in and tossed her in the kitchen. She glared at me balefully, then got revenge by leaping on top of the dryer, onto a pile of freshly folded laundry.

I turned to Howard and smiled my most encouraging smile.

"So. You said over the phone that you wanted me to write a letter for you?"

He blinked, as if hearing this news for the first time.

"You did want me to write a letter, didn't you?"

He picked at a scab on his knuckle. "That's right."

"What kind of letter? A consumer complaint? The airlines lose your luggage?" (I get a lot of those.)

"No." He was staring down at my hardwood floors, avoiding my glance.

"Look, Howard. I can't write a letter for you if you don't tell me what it's about."

He mumbled something to one of the grooves in my hardwood floor. It sounded something like "luvveter."

"What?"

At last, he looked up at me.

"A love letter. I want you to write a love letter."

The words "*You* have a girlfriend?" shot out of my mouth before I could stop myself. "I mean, you have a *girlfriend!* How nice!" I added quickly, hoping he hadn't noticed my momentary lack of couth.

"Not exactly."

"Oh. Is it a boyfriend? Nothing wrong with that. Not at all."

"No, no. It's a girl. It's just that she's not my girlfriend. In fact, I've never actually spoken to her.

But I know that I love her. With all my heart and soul."

Oh, jeez. I smiled woodenly. My first stalker.

"So. Tell me. Who is she, this love of yours?"

He whipped out a ragged newspaper clipping from his wallet and thrust it at me.

"Her name," he said reverently, "is Stacy."

I looked down at a picture of a lethal blonde in a black leotard. The caption read, "S. Lawrence Named New Sports Club Aerobics Instructor."

"She teaches aerobics at my gym."

Guys are amazing, aren't they? You take your average geeky woman. Sure, she may fantasize about Tom Cruise, but does she actually expect to wind up dating him? Of course not. She knows she's going to wind up with a guy named Norm with love handles and hairy knuckles. Men, on the other hand, are totally delusional. I'll bet there are thousands of short, fat, bald guys convinced they could be dating Heather Locklear if only they knew her phone number.

I looked down at the blonde in the clipping, with her hard-as-nails eyes, deep tan, and perfect body. Poor Howard didn't stand a chance.

"Look, Howard. I'm not so sure it's a wise idea to write a love letter to someone you don't even know."

"It doesn't have to be a love letter, exactly. I want you to write her something that will make her want to date me."

You want a miracle? I thought. *Go to Lourdes.*

"How about I write you a resume instead? You happy at your job?"

But he wasn't budging. "I want you to write a letter to Stacy."

"Okay," I said, forcing a smile, "tell me a little about yourself."

He stared at me blankly.

"What do you do for a living?"

"I'm an insurance adjuster."

Ouch. Not much excitement there.

"Hobbies?"

"I watch TV a lot."

"That's it?"

"Well," he said, obviously saving the best for last, "Mom and I collect chopsticks from Chinese restaurants."

I sighed deeply. I knew I had to turn down the job. It wouldn't be fair to take Howard's money for something I knew would never work out. If there's one thing I pride myself on, it's my integrity.

"Look, Howard. This isn't going to work."

"I'll pay you triple your usual fee."

I reached for my pad and pen.

"Is that Stacy with a 'y' or an 'ie'?"

Chapter Two

Okay, so I was a little low on integrity that week. I had bills to pay, and a costly Frappucino habit to support.

It's not cheap living in Beverly Hills. Not even when you live, like I do, on the wrong side of the tracks, south of Wilshire Boulevard. Wilshire is the dividing line in Beverly Hills. North of Wilshire, you're rich. South of Wilshire, you're not. And I'm south of Wilshire. So south, I'm practically in Mexico.

I live on a quiet tree-lined street dotted with duplexes. I've got a one-bedroom apartment with a working fireplace, hardwood floors, and an enviable location just up the street from a Starbucks. On the down side, there's the rent (high), the traffic (often impossible), and my neighbor Lance Venable (always impossible).

Lance lives next to me in the front unit of our duplex. A natty dresser with a headful of tight blond curls, Lance works at Neiman Marcus, selling ladies' shoes. I guess when you spend your days cramming bunions into Ferragamos you're bound to be a bit cranky.

The trouble with Lance is he's got Superman-quality hearing. The man hears sounds even dogs can't hear. Someone flushes the toilet in Pomona, and Lance hears it. Needless to say, Lance hears just about everything I do in my apartment. He hears my phone, he hears my hair dryer, he claims he can hear Prozac meowing to be fed. The only thing he doesn't hear are the sounds of me having sex in the bedroom. Mainly because there aren't any. But that's a whole other story. One I'd be glad to tell you about if I weren't already in the middle of telling you about Howard, the lovesick goofball.

When Howard left my apartment that afternoon, I knew I was deep into Mission Impossible territory. I noodled around on my computer for a while, trying to think what I could possibly write that would lure Stacy out on a date with Howard. The best I could come up with was:

"Dear Stacy, If you go out with me, I'll give you a million dollars. Yours sincerely, Howard Murdoch."

And frankly, I wasn't sure even that would work.

After an hour or two of intense thought, and seventeen trips to the refrigerator to see if anything interesting had shown up since the last time I looked, I came up with exactly nothing. So I put Howard's file aside and went back to work on a resume I'd been writing for a recent college graduate who'd majored in Parties and was now trying to give the impression that he'd actually attended some of his classes. It wasn't easy, but it was a damn sight easier than Howard.

At about six o'clock, I was interrupted by Prozac, wailing for her dinner. Poor darling hadn't eaten for at least an hour. I know I shouldn't give in to her constant demands for food, and every day I vow I'm going to limit her intake to just five meals a day, but I always wind up giving in after just a few pitiful meows.

After feeding Prozac her Savory Mackerel Feast, I hurried into the shower. I had a dinner date that night, and I wanted to look good.

I was in the middle of blow-drying my hair, trying to torture my natural curls into a sleek Jennifer Aniston do, when Lance started banging on the wall.

"Keep it down in there!"

I gritted my teeth and turned the dryer down to "low," wondering if I could possibly afford a hit man to puncture Lance's eardrums.

I got myself all gussied up in a pair of Ann Taylor slacks, J. Crew sweater, and K mart Control Top Pantyhose. I checked myself out in the mirror and saw that my freshly straightened hair was already beginning to frizz. In less than ten minutes, I'd gone from Jennifer Aniston to Shirley Temple. Just the look I was aiming for: a thirty-six-year-old moppet.

Oh, well. There was nothing I could do. If I didn't hurry, I'd be late for my date. I grabbed my purse and bent down to kiss Prozac good-bye. She licked my neck hungrily, no doubt searching for cat food hidden behind my ears.

Then I headed out the door, with a spring in my step, a curl in my hair, and mackerel-scented saliva on my neck.

I walked into the trendy restaurant on Melrose. You know the kind of place: where all the waiters

are actors, and the pesto flows like water. I looked
around the room. A handsome guy in a black
turtleneck sweater and wire-rimmed glasses waved
from his table. Unfortunately, he wasn't waving at
me, but at the stunning redhead behind me.

I headed over to where Kandi was sitting, waiting for me.

Kandi Tobolowski is an ex-New Yorker with envi-
ably straight hair and a great sense of humor
(which comes in handy when you're saddled with
a name like Kandi Tobolowsky).

I guess you could say Kandi is my best friend. We
met five years ago at a UCLA screenwriting class.
I'd just been through a messy divorce (are there
any other kind?) and was looking for a way to
stretch my creative muscles. Oh, who am I kidding?
I was looking for a way to get out of my apartment
one night a week.

Kandi had just moved out to L.A. from New York,
determined to make it in show biz. I've always been
drawn to New Yorkers. I like their edge, their impatience, their chutzpah. Most of all, I like the fact
that they never tell me to Have a Nice Day.

So when I saw Kandi in class that first night of the
summer session, tapping her feet impatiently and
muttering, "Jeez, it's like a sauna in here," I plopped
down next to her.

Our instructor was a bloated man with a greasy
ponytail who spent most of the semester trashing
our scripts and flirting with a sexy blonde in the
first row. Not that I blamed him for flirting. The
blonde was one heck of a good-looking guy.

One night the instructor was energetically trashing some poor shnook's script, something the
shnook had clearly been writing and rewriting for

most of his adult life. Kandi, glaring at the instructor with disgust, scribbled a note and handed it to me. It said, "Quelle asshole."

I knew then that Kandi was Best Friend material.

I made my way across the crowded restaurant and joined Kandi at a prized table she'd staked out by the window. She jumped up and hugged me happily. "Guess what, honey? I've met Mr. Right."

That's the crazy thing about Kandi. You'd think, coming from the mean streets of New York, she'd know the score about men. You'd think she'd have figured out by now that guys are like parking spaces (all the good ones are taken). But no, each time Kandi meets a new man, she's convinced she's met Mr. Right.

"Didn't you just meet Mr. Right last month?" I asked. "The crazy dentist, who took you out for dinner at the beach and then threatened to throw you off the Santa Monica pier?"

"That's ancient history. Wait'll you see this one. He's perfect. Just look at his fact sheet."

Kandi belongs to Foto-Date, one of those dating services that hands out fact sheets on prospective dates, listing all their vital statistics (none of which are verified), what they're looking for in a woman (Michelle Pfeiffer), and how they like to spend their free time (forget "romantic dinners" and "moonlight strolls on the beach"—what they really want is nonstop sex and dinner at your place).

I glanced down at the fact sheet.

"See? He's a doctor! In Beverly Hills! And look at his picture! Doesn't he look just like Antonio Banderas?"

I blinked in disbelief. Good heavens. He did look just like Antonio Banderas.

"He sounds too good to be true, doesn't he?"

"That should be a warning, Kandi."

"Oh, don't be such a worrywart. He's taking me to dinner. To a seafood place. Right on the beach."

"Better bring a life vest."

If I sound cynical, it's because I am. Three years with The Blob can do that to a gal. I call my ex-husband The Blob. And that's one of my more charitable nicknames.

I met The Blob at a coffeehouse in Santa Monica. He was writing the Great American Novel. With his dark, brooding eyes straight out of an El Greco painting, I thought he was the sensitive artist of my dreams. So, throwing caution—and my vibrator—to the winds, I married the guy.

Actually our marriage was great. It was the living together afterward that sucked. His Great American Novel turned out to be more like the Great American Paragraph. True, he spent endless hours at the computer. Most of them, I was eventually to discover, on the "Hot Babes in Thong Underwear" website. After a while, he abandoned his novel and retired to the sofa, where he proceeded to grow roots. When we finally divorced, I had to have the TV remote surgically removed from the palm of his hand.

"I'm starved," said Kandi, scarfing down the last of the focaccia bread. We looked around for our waiter and spotted him fawning over people clearly more important than us. Kandi finally managed to catch his eye.

"Oh, actor!" she called out. "We'd like some menus, please."

"Great," I groaned. "Now he's going to spit in our food."

"Don't be silly. They like it when you kid around."

Our waiter, a pretty young man with eyelashes to die for, stomped over to our table and hurled some menus in our general direction.

"Yeah, right. He's crazy about us."

Kandi waved away my sarcasm with a breadstick. "Honey," she said, "I've got fabulous news. Skip said he'd take a meeting with you. So think up some ideas for the cockroach."

In the five years since our UCLA course, Kandi had landed a job as a staff writer on *Beanie & the Cockroach,* a Saturday morning cartoon show about a short-order cook named Beanie who has a pet cockroach named Fred.

"I'm sorry, Kandi, but if I live to be a hundred, I won't have story ideas for a cockroach."

"It's easy. Come on. We'll brainstorm." She swiped a piece of focaccia from a passing busboy and chewed it thoughtfully. "I know. What if the cockroach starts dating a termite, and his mother is furious at him for dating out of his species? Or what if Beanie takes the cockroach with him on a fancy catering job, and highjinks ensue when the snooty guests find Fred on the salmon mousse?"

I smiled woodenly.

Compared to the cockroach, writing that letter for Howard suddenly didn't seem so bad.

Chapter
Three

Dear Stacy,

My name is Howard, and I'm one of the regulars in your Step Aerobics class. Although we've never actually spoken, for the past several months I've admired you from afar.

And so I'm writing to ask you out on a date.

I'm sure that a woman as beautiful as you probably has dozens of admirers. And I also realize that you don't even know me. But as my uncle Rupert always says, "Nothing ventured, nothing gained."

Your not-so-secret admirer,
Howard Murdoch

"But I don't have an uncle Rupert."

Howard sat across from me at my dining room table, tapping his foot in a nervous staccato on my hardwood floor. I couldn't help noticing that his fingernails were bitten to oblivion.

"Look, Howard," I said as gently as I could. "Let's face facts. Under ordinary circumstances, Stacy might not go out with you. After all, she's a very beautiful woman, and like I said in the letter, she's bound to have all sorts of guys vying for her attention."

(TRANSLATION: She'd turn you down so fast, your pens would be spinning in your pocket protector.)

"But if she thinks you're related to Rupert Murdoch, you might stand a chance."

Howard blinked, puzzled.

"Who's Rupert Murdoch?"

Good Lord. What planet was this guy from, anyway?

"Only one of the richest men in the world."

"But Stacy isn't the kind of girl who'd go out with a guy just because he's rich."

Right. And Oreos aren't fattening.

"Besides, if I say he's my uncle, isn't that lying?"

Prozac looked up from where she was napping on the dining table and shot me a look, as if to say, "Is this guy for real?" Or maybe she was saying, "When do we eat?" With cats, it's hard to tell.

"I prefer to think of it as a means to an end," I said.

"Won't she be mad when she finds out I'm not really Rupert Murdoch's nephew?"

"You can only hope by the time she learns the truth, she will have fallen in love with you."

"Gee, I don't know," said Howard, chewing on his lower lip. "Isn't there any other way to get her to go out with me?"

"Other than taking her hostage, I don't think so."

Poor Howard. He was so damned innocent, with his bulging brown eyes and polyester pants. If he wanted Stacy, he was going to have to lie. After all, we were in a town where lying is a way of life, and the truth is as rare as wrinkles in Malibu.

Howard looked at me with trusting eyes. "If you think it'll work . . ."

"I do," I said.

And much to my surprise, it did.

Three days later, Howard phoned me, barely able to contain his excitement.

"Stacy said yes! We're going out tonight. Can you believe it?"

Actually, I couldn't.

"That's wonderful, Howard."

"How can I thank you? Do you realize this will be the first time in my life I've ever had a date on Valentine's Day? Usually I just go to the movies with Mom."

Good Lord. Just when you think no one could possibly be any more pathetic than you, someone comes along and out-pathetics you.

I wished Howard the best of luck with Stacy, and got off the phone.

If I didn't hurry, I'd be late for my own Valentine's date. Surprised you, didn't I? Bet you thought I'd be sitting home alone with Soup for One. Well, you're wrong.

I gussied myself up and headed out the door for my hot date. With twelve senior citizens at the Shalom Retirement Home.

I volunteer once a week at the Shalom Retirement Home, teaching a memoir-writing class for seniors. It's just my way of contributing to the community and helping the elderly add a little meaning to their lives. Okay, okay. It's my way of getting out of my apartment one night a week.

When I first signed up for the gig, I thought I'd be hearing wonderful *Stones for Ibarra*-ish memories—exciting adventures, touching tales of meaningful relationships, and atmosphere-soaked descriptions of life at the beginning of the century. Instead, I got wooden travelogues about "My Trip to Israel" or equally leaden tributes to "My Son, the Orthodontist."

It's funny. Women of my generation will bare their souls to perfect strangers at the drop of an hors d'oeuvre. We'll complain about our parents, our lovers, our vaginal dryness. But the ladies of that generation (and most of my students are ladies) wouldn't dream of sharing anything negative about their private lives with the outside world. In my class, all the parents are loving, all the children are devoted, and all the dead husbands are up for sainthood.

In spite of their less than stirring memoirs, I'm really quite fond of these ladies. At seventy- and eighty-something—when many of their peers are sitting slack-jawed in front of Jerry Springer—they're taking out their pens and putting something down on paper each week (not easy at any age). I don't care if they don't share their innermost thoughts. I care that they show up at my class each week, still taking a whack at life.

I want to be like them when I grow up.

I got in my Corolla that Valentine's Day and headed east on Pico Boulevard. Traffic was a nightmare. Pedestrians were making better time than I was. The roads were clogged with gooey-eyed Valentine's couples on their way to dinner, giggling and flirting and necking at red lights. I hope they all caught gum diseases.

Disgusted with the traffic on Pico, I ducked onto a side street, where I whizzed along, if your definition of "whizzing" is stopping for nineteen stop signs. I finally pulled into the parking lot of the Shalom Retirement Home, a one-time apartment building now chopped up into one- and two-room "retirement suites."

I hurried into the conference room to find my students already seated, talking among themselves, complaining about the chicken at dinner (dry and tasteless—and such small portions). A few of them eschewed food criticism to scribble last-minute changes on their essays.

"Sorry I'm late, folks."

"That's okay, sweetie."

Mr. Goldman, the lone man in my class, winked at me. At least I think it was a wink. Mr. Goldman has a nervous tic, so I can never quite tell when he's winking or blinking.

As I sprinted over to my seat, I noticed an apple at the head of the conference table.

"For you, doll."

Mr. Goldman grinned broadly, exposing an impressive set of dentures.

Mrs. Pechter, a soft, powdery lady with bosoms the size of throw pillows, shook her head in disgust.

Of the dozens of women in the Shalom Retirement Home, Mr. Goldman had set his sights on a woman forty-eight years his junior—me. Here he was surrounded by women his own age and background, women he actually had something in common with. But no, he wanted someone young

enough to be his granddaughter. A common Los
Angeles malady, technically known as "The Michael
Douglas Syndrome."

"I polished it myself," he boasted, eyeing the
apple proudly.

"Yeah," added Mrs. Pechter, "with his sweater."

I glanced at Mr. Goldman's gravy-stained cardi-
gan and smiled weakly.

"Thank you, Mr. Goldman," I said, then turned
to the others. "Okay, who wants to read first this
week?"

I glanced at Mrs. Vincenzo, hoping she'd volunteer. A slender woman with a dancer's body and
long silken hair that she wore swept up on the crown
of her head in a wobbly bun, Bette Vincenzo was
the talent of the class. She was a rabbi's daughter
who'd rebelled against her Orthodox upbringing
by marrying a Catholic fireman. She told the stories of her life—if not always grammatically—with
refreshing candor. Unlike the other ladies, she never
worried about keeping up appearances when writing about her many marriages (four, so far), her
offbeat jobs, and her fondness for tequila.

I eyed her hopefully, and sure enough, she
whipped out a story, written boldly on looseleaf
paper with turquoise marker.

"When I was sixty-four," she began, "I got a job
as a ticket taker in a porno movie house. . . ."

What a dame. I was thirty-six, but compared to
her, I felt eighty-six. One of these days, as Mrs.
Pechter was fond of saying, I really was going to
have to "have a life."

After Mrs. Vincenzo finished her tale of life in
the porno biz, Mrs. Rubin read about her trip to
The Orient (paid for by her son, the doctor), and

Mrs. Zahler regaled us with tales of the late Mr. Zahler's charitable activities.

Finally, I could ignore it no longer—Mr. Goldman's eager hand, waving to be recognized.

"Okay, Mr. Goldman, why don't you read us what you've written."

He took out a depressingly thick wad of pages from his notebook and began reading the latest installment in his epic saga, "My Life as a Carpet Salesman."

In the story of his life, Mr. Goldman spared us no details. We heard about the ups. The downs. The good. And the bad. ("Area rugs—feh!") Like Mrs. Vincenzo, Mr. Goldman had no qualms about sharing the intimate moments of his life. Somewhere in every story, he wrote about what an exciting lover he'd been—always looking up from his pages to wink/blink at me.

Now Mr. Goldman was rambling on about the advent of broadloom. I looked around the table. Mrs. Pechter was nodding off already, not two paragraphs into his tale.

As Mr. G. thrilled us with the pros and cons of Scotch-garding, my mind started to wander. I thought of Mrs. Vincenzo and her life filled with lovers. What was wrong with me, anyway? Why couldn't I at least *try* to meet men? My last Valentine's date had been more than four years ago. With The Blob. If you can call it a date. He bought me a five-pound box of chocolates, ate it while I was getting dressed to go out for dinner, and then spent the rest of the night puking in the toilet bowl.

At last, Mr. Goldman ground to a halt. The ladies nudged each other awake, and we adjourned for the evening. Mr. Goldman asked me if I'd like to join him for a moonlight stroll around the parking lot.

"No, thanks," I said, hurrying out the door.

"Wait," he cried. "You forgot your apple."

Gritting my teeth, I walked back into the room.

"You sure you won't change your mind?" he said. "I'm one heck of a kisser."

"It's mighty tempting, but I'll pass."

"How about you come back and see me Saturday night? It's Mambo Mania night."

"Sorry, but I'm going to be busy."

"Doing what?"

"I don't know. I haven't decided yet."

"In other words, you're telling me you're not interested."

"Not in other words, Mr. Goldman. In those words."

He blinked in amazement. This time it was a blink, not a wink. Clearly he wasn't expecting such an overt rebuff.

"Okay, you don't have to hit me over the head with a hammer. I wasn't born yesterday. I get it. You're not interested."

He turned away from me and started gathering his papers with trembling liver-spotted hands.

I felt awful. What on earth had possessed me to speak to him so harshly?

"Look, Mr. Goldman, I'm sorry. I didn't mean to upset you."

He peered at me suspiciously.

"Really?"

"Really."

"Okay," he grinned, "so how about Sunday? You want to go to the movies? They're playing *The*

Sound of Music in the rec room. We can neck when they turn the lights down."

I grabbed my apple and ran.

I drove home and headed straight to where I always go when I'm stressed—the bathtub. With a pit stop at the refrigerator to pour myself a glass of wine. Okay, two glasses of wine.

I plopped some strawberry bath salts in the tub and sniffed with satisfaction as the room filled with berry-scented steam. Then I turned on the radio to a classical music station and sank down into the tub. I lay there, listening to Beethoven's *Moonlight Sonata* and sipping my bargain chardonnay, imported all the way from Fresno. I could feel the tension oozing out of my body. It was all quite divine, until my neighbor Lance Venable, he of the x-ray hearing, started banging on the wall.

"Keep it down, will you?"

With a sigh, I turned off the radio and plopped back into the tub. I tried humming the *Moonlight Sonata,* but somehow it didn't sound quite as snazzy as the London Philharmonic. After a while, Prozac wandered in and leaped up onto the toilet tank. She gazed down at me through slitted eyes, as if to say, "What fools these mortals be to get their bodies wet." Either that or, "Got any tuna?" Like I say, with cats, it's hard to tell.

I soaked for about forty-five minutes, until my fingertips were raisins and my hair had frizzed to the consistency of Brillo. Finally, when I'd licked the last drop of chardonnay from the glass, I hauled myself out of the tub.

I wrapped myself in a coffee-stained chenille

bathrobe that I'd owned since Ally McBeal was in junior high, and got into bed. I flicked on the TV with my remote and zapped around, checking out Today's Special Value on QVC, Lucy and Ethel at the candy factory, and an infomercial for an instrument of torture appropriately named the Ab Dominator.

Finally, I flipped to the news—just in time to see a skinny guy with a bobbing Adam's apple being taken into police custody. Wait a minute. I knew that skinny guy. It was Howard Murdoch. I sat up straight in bed. What the heck was Howard doing in police custody?

The TV reporter obligingly filled me in. My mild-mannered client, a guy so timid he was probably afraid of Count Chocula, was being arrested for the grisly murder of Westside aerobics instructor Stacy Lawrence.

Chapter Four

"**I** swear, I didn't do it."

I sat across from Howard in the visitors' room of the county jail, a stark, fluorescent-lit cavern that smelled like old oatmeal. It was the morning after Howard's arrest, and I'd driven over to see him. Needless to say, I felt responsible for his incarceration. If I hadn't written that stupid letter, Howard would never have had a date with Stacy in the first place.

Of course, it was possible he'd actually killed her. But I didn't believe it. Not for a minute. The TV reporter said Stacy had been bludgeoned to death. I just couldn't picture Howard in the act of bludgeoning. I mean, he's the kind of guy who needs help with a twist-top cap.

Howard sat behind a fingerprint-smudged glass partition, his skinny body lost in the voluminous folds of his orange jailhouse jumpsuit. He gnawed at his lower lip, his eyes wide with bewilderment and disbelief.

"What on earth happened?" I said into the prison telephone.

"I don't know." He shook his head. "I showed up at her apartment, and she was dead."

"How did you get in?"

"The door was open; I just walked in."

"And then?"

He shut his eyes, replaying the scene in his mind.

"The apartment was dark. I called out to Stacy, but she didn't answer. I thought maybe she was in the shower, but I didn't hear any water running. I called out to her again. Still no answer. For a minute, I wondered if this was her way of standing me up, but that didn't make any sense. Why wouldn't she just come to the door and tell me to get lost? By then I was starting to get worried, so I went down the hall to her bedroom."

He shuddered at the memory of what happened next.

"I saw her lying there, in the dark. I was so close to her, I could smell her perfume. I remember thinking how nice it smelled. I called her name, but she still didn't answer. Finally, I got up my courage and turned on the light. And that's when I saw all the blood."

Tears welled in his eyes. "Oh, God, it was awful."

"Did you call the police?"

"No, I tried to give her artificial respiration. I thought maybe I could save her. But I couldn't. And then the police came and found me, with her blood all over me."

"Who called the police?"

"One of the neighbors. The lady next door. I told the cops I didn't do it, but I could tell they didn't believe me." He was chewing on his lower lip so hard, I was surprised it wasn't bleeding. "My mom's so upset, I'm afraid she's going to have a heart attack."

"Don't worry, Howard. You can't go to jail for something you didn't do."

"But I am in jail."

He had a point there.

"Have you called an attorney?"

"Yeah, I found one in the Yellow Pages."

Oh, great. I could see it now. The judge asks Howard, *"How do you plead?"* And Howard, thanks to the crackerjack advice he gets from his Yellow Pages attorney, answers, *"On my knees, Your Honor."*

"Don't you know any other attorney?"

"Just my cousin Bruce, but he's been disbarred."

I smiled what I hope was an encouraging smile. "I'm sure everything's going to be okay," I lied.

I waved good-bye through the fingerprints in the glass partition and left him sitting there, still holding the phone to his ear, a geek caught in the headlights.

I was walking down the corridor, trying to get the smell of oatmeal out of my nostrils, when I felt a tap on my shoulder.

"Ms. Austen?"

I turned around and saw a cop who couldn't have been more than twelve, trying to look stern.

"Detective Rea would like to see you."

Minutes later, I was being ushered into the office of Detective Timothy Rea. Luckily, it didn't smell of oatmeal. It did, however, smell of cigarettes and gym socks.

Detective Rea was a tall, good-looking guy with reddish blond hair and ears just a little too big for his head. He reminded me of Joey Ross, a kid I went to elementary school with. Joey was a world-class wiseass, always challenging the teachers and acting like he knew all the answers. And the irritating thing about Joey was that he really *did* know all the answers. He was a smart guy, and he never let you forget it.

Detective Rea looked just like Joey during a pop quiz.

"Have a seat, Ms. Austen."

He gestured to a chair that had clearly been around since Los Angeles belonged to the Spaniards.

"Howard tells me you helped him write this letter."

He held up the dratted letter.

I nodded weakly.

"Did you know he was lying about being Rupert Murdoch's nephew? We checked with Mr. Murdoch, and he says he has no nephew named Howard."

"Actually, that was my idea," I said, shame bubbling to my cheeks. "Howard didn't want to lie. I talked him into it. It's all my fault."

"Then maybe we should book you as an accessory," Rea joked. At least, I hoped he was joking.

"Look," I said, "I know I don't have any training in this sort of thing, but I'm a very good judge of character, and I just can't believe Howard is capable of murder. I mean, if he wanted to kill Stacy, why would he leave a paper trail? Why wouldn't he have just followed her home from the gym and killed her in an alley or something?"

Detective Rea looked at me with appraising eyes.

"You're right."

I sighed with relief. Obviously Howard's arrest was all a terrible mistake. I could go home and soak in the tub and forget the whole thing ever happened.

"You don't have any training whatsoever in police matters. And if you'll pardon my saying so, you don't know what you're talking about. We found Howard covered in his victim's blood, holding the ThighMaster."

"The ThighMaster?"

"The murder weapon."

"Stacy was bludgeoned to death with a Thigh-Master?"

He nodded somberly. "The woman in Apartment Seven heard Howard screaming and called the police."

"But that doesn't mean he killed her. Maybe somebody else was in the apartment before him. Maybe that person ran off when he heard Howard coming. Did you look for footprints outside Stacy's patio?"

"Yes, we looked for footprints. We often do technical stuff like that here at the police department."

"And? Did you find any?"

"As a matter of fact, we did. The gardener's. One Chuy Sandoval, who at the time of the murder was home having dinner with his wife and four kids."

"What about the other neighbors? Did any of them hear anything unusual?"

"Aside from Howard screaming, no."

Rea picked up a file from his desk.

"Did you know your client has a history of mental illness?"

Uh-oh.

"He does?"

He nodded, the same sure-of-himself grin on his face that Joey Ross had in the final round of our fifth grade spelling bee.

"He's been hospitalized twice."

"For what?"

"Depression and anorexia."

"Anorexia?" I snorted. "Sounds like the mental history of a killer, all right."

"Well, I think he did it." Rea lit a cigarette and blew a plume of smoke in my direction. "Unfortunately for Howard, I'm the cop on the case. And you're not."

He smiled smugly. And suddenly I remembered the final round of the fifth grade spelling bee. It was Joey Ross's turn. The word was "euphemistic." And Joey spelled it with an "f."

For once in his life, Joey was wrong. Just as wrong, I was certain, as Detective Timothy Rea.

Chapter
Five

I left Detective Rea's office in a pissy mood and headed back to the visitors' room at the county jail.

"What's Stacy's address?" I asked when Howard was once again seated across from me in his smudgy glass cage.

"She lives in Westwood." A flash of pain swept over his face. "I mean, she lived in Westwood. A place called Bentley Gardens."

"You remember the exact address?"

"1622 Bentley. Why do you want to know?"

"I want to pay a little visit," I said, "to the scene of the crime."

Five minutes later, I was on the freeway, heading over to Westwood. I wanted to talk to Stacy's neighbor in Apartment Seven, the lady who'd heard Howard screaming. If she heard Howard, maybe she'd heard something else, something that would point me in the direction of the true killer.

Wait a minute, you're probably asking yourself. I'm a freelance writer, right? So how come I was talking like V.I. Warshawski? That's just what I was asking myself that day as I headed over to Stacy's place. What on earth did I think I was doing? Surely, the police had already questioned everyone. If there were any pertinent facts to be discovered, they would have discovered them.

Then I thought of Detective Rea, and that smug grin on his face, and I knew exactly why I was heading over to Westwood.

Stacy lived on a leafy street a couple of miles from the UCLA campus. Bentley Gardens was a small but well-maintained building, with purple pansies bordering the patch of lawn out front.

I parked my car and headed up a flagstone path to a security intercom. I checked out the building directory and found Apartment Seven. The name on the buzzer said "E. Zimmer." I was just about to ring, when I suddenly wondered: What the heck was I going to say to E. Zimmer? *"Hello, I'm a friend of the man who was arrested for killing your neighbor."* I don't think so.

I was standing there trying to figure out a plan of attack when I saw a Jeep pull into the building's carport. A clean-cut guy in his thirties got out and started taking suitcases from the trunk of his car. I pretended to be looking for something in my purse as he came up the path. He smiled at me absently, then took out his keys and let himself in. I couldn't help noticing his eyes, a beautiful Aidan Quinn blue.

"Here, let me hold the door for you," I said, as he juggled his suitcases.

"Thanks." He flashed me another smile, this one of slightly higher wattage than the first, and made his way in. Needless to say, I slipped in right behind him.

Seven apartments surrounded a postage stamp–sized pool in the courtyard of Bentley Gardens. The pool was deserted, except for a few plastic chaises scattered along its rim.

Mr. Blue Eyes let himself into Apartment Four. I tried to look like I knew where I was going as I scanned the doors, looking for Number Seven. Fortunately, Blue Eyes was too busy schlepping suitcases to pay much attention to me.

I walked past Number Six and saw yellow police tape crisscrossing the door. Obviously Stacy's place. I approached Number Seven, and could hear the low hum of a TV inside.

I had decided on a plan of attack and was just about to knock on E. Zimmer's door, when I heard, in a gruff Russian accent: "Who are you?"

I turned to see a dark butterball of a man, glaring at me suspiciously.

I did a little mini-glare of my own. Sounding a lot braver than I felt, I countered, "And you are . . . ?"

"Daryush Kolchev, Building Manager."

"I'm with the press," I said, putting my plan of attack into action. And it wasn't a total lie, either. Back in high school, I was a star reporter for the *Lincoln High Tattler.* Okay, so I wasn't a star reporter. But I did write some pretty angry Letters to the Editor.

The Russian eyed me skeptically. "Oh?"

"I'm with *The Times.*"

I flashed him a press card. Okay, so it wasn't a press card. It was my Bloomingdale's charge card, but I was hoping he wouldn't know the difference.

"*Los Angeles Times* reporter, he came last night, with other media peoples."

"Oh," I said, not missing a beat, "not the *Los Angeles Times. The New York Times.*"

"I have cousin in New York. Yakov Kolchev. You know him?"

"No, can't say I do."

"Okay," he said, brushing back the few remaining strands of hair on his head. "I talk to you. I tell you just what I told other media peoples last night. Stacy Lawrence, she was angel from heaven. Such a smile. And never once late with her rent. If all my tenants pretty and nice like her, I be happy man."

Clearly, Howard hadn't been the only one with a crush on Stacy.

"Hey, how come you're not writing this down?"

"Not necessary. I have a photographic memory. It's all in here," I said, tapping my forehead. If I told one more lie, my nose would start growing. "Did you see anything unusual last night? Anybody suspicious?"

"Sure. I see someone suspicious."

"Who?" I asked, eagerly.

"The guy they arrested. He look very suspicious to me."

"See anyone else?"

"No, my wife and I were in apartment watching television. Home Shopping. We buy genuine cubic zirconia. Only $19.95, plus shipping and handling."

"Well, that's swell. Now if you'll excuse me, I want to talk to Ms. Zimmer."

"Better you than me," he said, rolling his eyes and gesturing toward Number Seven. "That Elaine Zimmer. Miserable lady. Always complaining. Tenants like her, I can do without. Not pretty and peppy like Stacy Lawrence."

His eyes misted over at the mention of Stacy's name. But he didn't stay sentimental for long.

"Be sure you spell my name right for *New York Times*. D-A-R-Y-U-S-H K-O-L-C-H-E-V. Here. I give you card."

He reached into his pants pocket and pulled out a grease-stained business card. "I'm good handyman. You call if something breaks."

Just then a large woman stepped out from an apartment at the other end of the courtyard.

"Daryush. Come quick. Is diamond bracelet on television. Free shipping and handling!"

Mr. Kolchev thrust his greasy business card into my hand and scurried off to join his wife.

As I stood there watching him, I couldn't help thinking that Daryush Kolchev had been quite fond of Stacy Lawrence. Maybe a little too fond. And I couldn't help wondering if Daryush's rather large, unattractive wife was the jealous type. Jealous enough, perhaps, to bash her rival's head in with a ThighMaster?

Chapter
Six

A famous philosopher (either Aristotle or Judith Krantz, I forget who) once said about being a woman in Los Angeles: If you're blonde and beautiful, you're interchangeable. If you're not, you're invisible.

Elaine Zimmer was one of the invisible ones.

She answered her doorbell, a short, squat woman in a nurse's uniform.

"Yes?"

She looked at me with an intimidating blend of suspicion and impatience.

"Hi," I said, flashing a smile and my Bloomie's card. "I'm with *The Times*." It worked so well with Daryush, I figured I'd give it another shot.

But Elaine was a lot smarter than Daryush.

"That's not a press card. That's a Bloomingdale's charge card."

"Oh?" I faked surprise. "Well, I'm sure I've got it in here somewhere." I rummaged through my purse, looking for my nonexistent press card. "Gosh, I must've left it at home. I changed wallets this morning. You know how that is."

"No, I don't know how that is."

She eyed me skeptically and started to shut the door.

"Look, you can call my editor if you don't believe me. Mark Simms, 213-555-3876." I figured if I was going to bluff, I might as well bluff on a grand scale. Mark Simms was my gynecologist.

Elaine headed for her telephone, the pants of her two-piece uniform straining at the seams. "What was that number?"

"Forget it," I said, slipping into the apartment behind her. "I'm not with the press. I'm here on behalf of my client, Howard Murdoch."

"Oh. The kid who killed Stacy."

"That hasn't been proven yet."

"For crying out loud, they found him covered with her blood."

"That still doesn't mean he killed her."

"Yeah, right," she said, ushering me toward the door. "Forgive me if my heart isn't brimming over with sympathy for Mr. Rich."

"Mr. Rich?"

"I heard he's Rupert Murdoch's nephew. Probably a spoiled brat."

"He's not Rupert Murdoch's nephew. I can swear to that."

"But what about his BMW?"

"Howard doesn't have a BMW."

"I saw one parked outside last night. A big black one. I assumed it was his. We don't get many BMWs on this block. This is definitely a Toyota neighborhood."

"Look, Ms. Zimmer, I can assure you Howard is

far from rich and far from spoiled. He works as an insurance adjuster and lives with his mother."

She thought this over and seemed to soften. Empathy from one of life's underdogs for another.

"You want some coffee?" she offered. "I was just fixing myself some."

"I'd love it."

I followed her to her cramped kitchen. Her apartment was small: living room, matchbox kitchen, and what I assumed was a bedroom down the hall.

The coffee smelled great. She poured it into UCLA mugs, and we sat at a pine table in her "dining nook," a tiny alcove jammed between the living room and the front door.

"So who are you, really?" she said, stirring Sweet'n Low into her coffee.

"An associate of Howard's. He's my client."

"You his lawyer?"

"No, his writer."

"His writer?"

"He hired me to write a letter that would convince Stacy to go on a date with him. Unfortunately for him, I took the assignment."

"You write letters that get people dates?" she asked, a glint of interest in her eyes.

"Most of the time I write resumes and brochures. Stuff like that. Anyhow, I was wondering if you saw or heard anything unusual last night."

"Just your client, screaming his head off."

"You didn't hear any cries from Stacy? Any indication that she was being murdered?"

"No. I was watching TV, though. There could've been some noise that I wouldn't have heard with the television on."

"So you heard Howard screaming and called the cops."

"First, I went next door to see what was going on. The door was open. Howard was in the bedroom, holding the ThighMaster, blood all over him. He was totally out of it. I don't even think he knew I was there. I could see right away Stacy was dead. Being an RN, I know about those things."

"A nurse," I nodded, trying to look impressed. "Where do you work?"

"UCLA. Psychiatric ward."

"Really?" I could easily picture her wrestling a patient into a straightjacket.

"Anyhow," she went on, "I saw that Stacy was dead, so that's when I called the cops. Want a Mallomar?"

I could tell she wanted one, so I said, "Sure."

"Be right back." She disappeared into her kitchen, and I looked around the tiny apartment. The place was crammed with white wicker and delicate floral prints. An interesting decorating choice. Nurse Ratched meets Laura Ashley.

I glanced over by the front door and saw a basket of laundry waiting to be washed. My eyes were drawn to a rust-colored stain on one of the blouses. From where I was sitting, it looked a heck of a lot like blood. Of course, it could have been spaghetti sauce, or strawberry margarita mix. It was hard to tell for sure.

"Here we go."

Elaine was back with a bag of cookies. She held it out, and I took one.

"So," I said, as she bit into a Mallomar with relish, "what was Stacy like?"

"World-class bitch," she said through cookie crumbs, chocolate gathering in the corners of her mouth.

"Really?"

"Sweet as pie if you were someone who could do her any good. Treated you like shit if you couldn't. Men loved her, of course. Blond hair, big boobs. That's what men really want. Forget all that crap about inner beauty, it's what's on the outside that counts."

She was right, of course. Life isn't fair, especially to short, stocky nurses with a fondness for chocolate.

"Your manager, Mr. Kolchev, sure seemed to be crazy about her."

Her face flushed with anger. "That moron," she spat out. "I ought to sue him. He gave Stacy that apartment, when it belonged to me."

"What do you mean?"

"The apartment next door. I told him years ago I wanted it. 'The minute it's vacant, I want it,' I told him. It's a big corner unit. With a den, and a terrace. Daryush promised he'd give it to me. Then two weeks ago, the lady who was living there died, and he gave it to Stacy."

She reached for another Mallomar.

"She was only living in the building a year, for crying out loud. I've been here for ten. Stacy didn't deserve that apartment. I did!"

Her face was bright red, suffused with rage. Frankly, I was a little spooked. I made a mental note to never have a nervous breakdown at the UCLA psychiatric ward.

"I guess I'd better be going now," I said, a little too brightly. "Thanks so much for your help."

"Sure," she said, normal again, as if she'd just woken from a bad dream.

And as she walked me to the door, I asked myself: Could Elaine Zimmer have been angry enough to kill Stacy over an apartment? Stranger things have happened in the wacky world of Los Angeles real estate.

She hesitated a moment before opening the door to let me out. My stomach lurched. Had she somehow sensed that I suspected her of killing Stacy? Was she about to bump me off with a UCLA coffee mug?

She smiled a tentative smile. "Those letters you write, to get people dates. You think you could write one for me?"

Thank God. She didn't want to kill me. Like most of the women in Los Angeles, all she wanted was a date.

"Sorry. I'm no longer in the love-letter business."

"How about Personals ads?" she asked hopefully. "You do those?"

"Nope," I lied. "Afraid not."

"That's too bad." She sighed, and opened the door.

I felt sorry for her. Poor thing probably hadn't had a date since the Carter administration. But no way was I going to get involved in someone's love life. Not again. Not after what happened with Howard. I thanked her for her time and scooted out the door. On my way out, I shot a furtive glance at the stained blouse in the laundry basket.

Sure looked like blood to me.

Back out in the courtyard, the sun was shining, the birds were chirping, and the breeze was breezing. It was all so darn idyllic; you'd never dream a young woman had recently been bludgeoned to death on the premises.

I stared at the police tape crisscrossed in front of Stacy's door and wondered if the door could possibly be open. I doubted it, but what the heck. I reached through the tape, and jiggled the doorknob. Just as I'd thought, it was locked.

I started to walk away when suddenly it occurred to me: I'd left my fingerprints at the scene of the crime. What sort of an idiot was I, anyway? Detective Rea had made that snide joke about arresting me. What if they found my prints on the doorknob and hauled me off to jail?

I rummaged through my purse for a Kleenex, then raced back to the door to wipe my fingerprints away. I was standing there, rubbing the doorknob, picturing myself in one of those unflattering orange jumpsuits, when I heard someone approaching. I quickly stashed my tissue in my pocket and turned to see Mr. Blue Eyes. I smiled feebly, trying to look as law abiding as possible.

"Hi." He smiled, his blue eyes crinkling in a most attractive way. "Are you from the police?"

"Yes," I lied. Well, it wasn't a total lie. After all, I'd just come from police headquarters, hadn't I?

"What's going on?"

"There's been a murder."

"You're kidding."

"Stacy Lawrence was murdered in her bed last night," I said in my most cop-like manner.

"My God, that's terrible," he said, running his fingers through a shock of thick, sandy hair. "But I don't get it. Stacy doesn't live in Number Six. Her apartment's across the courtyard."

"Not anymore. Apparently the victim moved into Six after the former tenant died."

(Notice how I said "the victim" instead of "Stacy"? Very coppish, *n'est ce pas?* I couldn't wait to work "perpetrator" into a sentence.)

"But I thought Elaine Zimmer was supposed to get this apartment."

"So did Elaine."

"Wow, she must've been steamed," he said.

At least, that's what I think he said. I wasn't paying all that much attention. Somehow I found myself staring at those blue eyes that crinkled at the corners when he laughed. *What the hell was I doing?* I scolded myself. After my ghastly marriage to The Blob, hadn't I sworn off men forever—or at least until I found one capable of asking for directions?

We were standing there, him talking to me and me staring at him, when suddenly a piercing scream filled the air.

"Whoops," he said. "My teakettle. Gotta run."

"Wait! I'd like to ask you some questions."

(Like, are you seeing anyone? Do you snore after sex? Do you hog the remote?)

"All right," he said, motioning me to his apartment. "Follow me."

His apartment was, as they say in decorating circles, eclectic. He had sleek minimalist pieces alongside time-worn antiques. If I had tried something like that, it would have looked ghastly. But his place looked terrific.

He settled me down on his minimalist sofa, while he brewed up some tea in the kitchen. First coffee, now tea—my bladder was getting quite a workout.

"By the way," he said, coming out from the kitchen

with a pot of steaming oolong, "my name's Cameron. Cameron Bannick."

"Jaine Austen."

He settled his lanky body into an armchair across from me. "Love your books."

"That's Jaine with an 'i.'"

"Well, Detective Austen," he said, "I'm happy to answer any questions I can, but I don't know how helpful I'm going to be. I've been away all month."

Thank God. That meant he couldn't possibly have had anything to do with the murder. Which meant we could start dating and get married and have a passel of kids with crinkly blue eyes.

"I've been on a business trip."

Solvent, too. Thanks again, God.

"Up in San Francisco, buying antiques for my shop."

Okay, cancel the wedding. The guy was obviously of the gay persuasion. Great decorator. Impeccable taste. Owns an antiques shop. You don't have to be Stephen Hawking to figure that one out.

"So," he said, "what would you like to know?"

Why are the good ones always gay? That's what I wanted to know. But what I actually asked was: "Do you know anyone in the building who might want to kill Stacy Lawrence?"

"Only Elaine, for cheating her out of that apartment. I'm kidding, of course. Elaine has a temper, but I can't believe she'd actually kill Stacy."

"What about the other tenants?"

"The Garibaldis in Number Two are in their eighties. Mr. Garibaldi uses a walker, and Mrs. Garibaldi isn't exactly doing handsprings. I doubt they'd have the strength to kill her. There's Janet

Yoshida in Number Three—she's a medical student at UCLA. Very quiet. Hardly ever here. I don't think any of them had much to do with Stacy. The only one she was close with was Marian."

"Marian?"

"The tenant who lived in Number Six before Stacy. She died about three weeks ago. I was in San Francisco at the time." He sighed deeply. "She was a terrific lady, and a good friend of mine."

He picked up a framed picture from the coffee table and looked at it fondly.

"That's us, last year on her birthday," he said, handing me the picture. "I took her to the Conga Room."

"The Conga Room? Isn't that one of those terminally hip clubs for twenty-somethings with multiple body-piercings?"

Cameron smiled. "That's where Marian wanted to go. She was quite a pistol."

I looked down at the picture and saw a heavily made-up woman in her seventies with youthful shoulder-length blond hair. Think Kim Basinger, with liver spots. I could tell that in her heyday Marian had been a knockout, but by the time this picture was taken, she was far from her heyday. Cameron sat beside her in the photo, smiling into the camera and holding her hand.

Exhibit A, Your Honor. Handsome young man, on a date with woman old enough to be his grandmother. If I'd had any fleeting hopes that Cameron was straight, that picture pretty much killed them.

"Stacy got a kick out of Marian," Cameron said. "You see, Marian had been an actress back in the forties and fifties. Made a lot of B movies. *Abbott & Costello Meet Each Other.* Stuff like that. She had a lot of terrific Hollywood war stories, and Stacy liked to pump her for advice."

"So Stacy wanted to be an actress?"

"She was blond. She was beautiful. She thought her navel was the center of the universe. Sure, she wanted to be an actress."

"And Marian was fond of Stacy?"

"She was flattered by her attention. Stacy reminded Marian of herself when she was young."

"Did Marian ever mention anyone in Stacy's life who might have perpetrated the crime?" (Yes! I worked in "perpetrated"!)

"You mean, like a jealous lover or something?"

"Exactly."

"Stacy dated a lot. Plenty of boyfriends du jour. She was going hot and heavy with an actor for a while. I saw him at the pool a couple of times. I couldn't help noticing he was a very handsome guy."

I'll bet you couldn't.

"The macho type, very muscular. Could probably bench-press a refrigerator. He seemed crazy about Stacy. But I guess he wasn't successful enough for her, because eventually she threw him over for someone else. Some hotshot agent."

Hmm. Spurned ex-boyfriend. Sounded promising.

"Anyone else who might have held a grudge?"

Cameron laughed. "You'll have to take a number on that one. Stacy was a bitch. Lots of people resented her."

"Like for instance?"

"There was a girlfriend of hers at the health club. Another aerobics instructor. I can't remember her name. Iris, or Violet. Some flower name.

Anyhow, she and Stacy were best friends, until Stacy made a play for her boyfriend, the hotshot agent. Stacy eventually managed to steal him away. So it's just a wild and crazy guess, but I'd say the former best friend is holding a bit of a grudge."

Betrayed best friend. Rich agent-lover. Two more juicy suspects. I made mental note to check out the LA Sports Club.

"If you couldn't help her in some way," Cameron said, "Stacy had no use for you. She once came into my shop looking for an étagère. She saw one she liked. When I wouldn't go down on the price, she got all pissy and barely spoke to me after that.

"Anyhow, lots of people didn't like her. I have no idea if any of them was angry enough to kill her."

"Were you?"

"Hell, no," he said, shaking his head at the absurdity of the notion. "Stacy meant nothing to me, one way or the other. She was definitely not my type."

That's for sure. Wrong gender.

"More tea?" He held out the pot.

"No, thanks. I'm fine."

He put down the teapot, and then, before I knew what was happening, he was actually saying, "Look, if you're not doing anything Wednesday night, maybe you'd like to catch a movie."

"With you?"

"Yeah." He grinned. "With me. They're playing one of Marian's old films at a revival theater in Silver Lake."

I'm afraid I just sat there, gulping, for an unattractive beat or two. Was Cameron Bannick, he of the glorious blue eyes, actually asking me out on a

date? Was it possible he wasn't gay, after all? That
he was simply a breathtaking stud with an affinity
for armoires?

"I probably shouldn't be asking you out on a
date. I don't know if the department would approve."

"What department?"

"The police department."

"Oh, right."

"So, how about it? Are we on for the movies?"

Somehow I managed to nod yes.

Chapter
Seven

My heart was pounding. My pulse was racing. And my palms were sweating. No, it wasn't sex. Or a heart attack. It was Starbucks. I swear, they put enough caffeine in their lattes to jump-start a diesel truck.

I was sitting across from Kandi, taking cautious sips of a mocha latte, listening to Kandi let off steam. And she was plenty steamed. In fact, I couldn't decide who was letting off more steam—Kandi or the espresso machine.

Kandi's date with the Antonio Banderas look-alike had been an utter disaster. Which I could have predicted. Men who look like Antonio Banderas don't need to join Foto-Date.

"The guy was short and fat and wore a toupee so obvious it practically had the price tag still on it."

"Where on earth did he get that picture he sent you?"

"From Antonio Banderas's fan club."

"You mean, the picture he sent you was actually Antonio Banderas?"

"Do you believe the nerve of that guy?" she said, tearing her napkin into angry shreds. "When I asked him if sending out Antonio Banderas's photo wasn't just a tad dishonest, he said, 'Of course not. After all, I look just like him.'"

"You're kidding."

"I was so upset, I practically choked on my Chicken McNuggets."

"He took you to McDonald's? Wasn't he supposed to take you to a restaurant on the beach?"

"Yeah, right. The closest I got to the water that night was the ladies' room, where I spent a good twenty minutes trying to escape through an overhead window."

"You poor thing."

"And remember how he said he was a doctor? He's a doctor, all right. Of phrenology. He reads the lumps on people's heads."

"You're kidding."

"He shares office space with a psychic named Wamsutta."

She drank the last of her espresso with an angry slurp.

"I've had it with Foto-Date. I should have known better than to sign up with a dating service that advertises in the *National Enquirer.*"

"Look, I hate to say I told you so—"

"Then don't," she said, grabbing my napkin. Having already ripped hers to shreds, she now began to mutilate mine.

"And if all that weren't bad enough," she moaned, "the cockroach has a hernia."

"What?"

"Carl, the actor who plays Freddie the cockroach on *Beanie & The Cockroach,* has a serious hernia problem, so we're going to have to shut down production for a whole week. And we're way behind on scripts as it is. I don't suppose you've come up with any cockroach stories?"

"No, the cockroach muse hasn't struck."

She shot me a dirty look, then flounced over to the counter. Minutes later she came back with a chocolate chip muffin the size of a Volkswagen.

"Here," she said, cutting it in two. "Have half."

"I can't. Really. If my thighs get any bigger, I'll have to rent them out as condos."

"C'mon. It's a muffin. Muffins are healthy."

"There's no way I'm eating this muffin," I said, grabbing my half. We sat and chewed companionably for a minute or two.

"Oh, well," Kandi said, obviously mellowed out by her chocolate fix. "The cockroach's hernia will heal, and I'll live to date again. Which reminds me. I heard of a great new way to meet guys— Christie's auction house."

The woman is tireless in her search for a mate. Utterly tireless.

"The place is loaded with eligibles. The script supervisor on *Beanie* met her fiancé there. A stockbroker. They were bidding against each other for a painting. He got the painting, and she got him. I'm sending away for their auction schedule. We'll go together."

"I don't think so. Those kind of ritzy places intimidate me."

"Don't be silly. You've got to start dating one of these days."

"Actually, I am dating."

Kandi put down her half of the muffin. "You are?"

"Well, not exactly dating, but I do have a date."

"With who?"

"Someone I met while I was investigating a murder."

"A murder? Oh, my God. Tell me all about it."

And I did.

"I don't believe it," she said, when I was through. "You've been impersonating a cop?"

"And a newspaper reporter."

"You'd better be careful or you'll wind up in His 'n Hers jail cells with Howard."

"Oh, come on. They don't arrest you for telling little white lies."

"Just be careful, will you? This whole thing sounds dangerous to me."

She was right, of course. It was dangerous. And I realized, much to my surprise, that the danger was a turn-on. For the first time in a long time I had some adrenaline pumping through my veins alongside Ben & Jerry's Chunky Monkey. And it felt good.

"I can't believe you're dating one of the suspects."

"I told you. We're not really dating. We're just going to a movie together. And he's not really a suspect. He was away in San Francisco at the time of the murder."

"That's what he says. There's a crazy new invention called an airplane that whisks people from San Francisco to Los Angeles in no time at all."

She had a point there. A point I hadn't considered.

"Besides," she said, "if you ask me, he's gay."

"You think so?"

"Of course he's gay. Antiques dealer. Fabulous apartment. Platonic relationship with an older woman. Taking you to a campy movie in Silver Lake, a neighborhood with more gays per square foot than a Bette Midler concert. It's all Classic Homosexual."

Now it was my turn to rip a napkin to shreds. Kandi was right. How could I have been stupid enough to think that Cameron was interested in me romantically? I was a Marian-substitute. Nothing more.

And what if he *had* flown to L.A. the night of the murder? It would have been easy enough to fly in, kill Stacy, and fly back up to San Francisco. And then get in his car and drive back to L.A. the next day, just in time to flash a blue-eyed smile at a dopey writer pretending to be a cop.

I downed the rest of my mocha latte in a single gulp, wishing it were Scotch.

The next day I called Cameron and told him I had to check on his whereabouts the night of the murder. Not that I believed in the slightest that he had anything to do with the murder, I assured him. It was strictly routine cop stuff.

"Sure thing," he said, "I understand. I was staying at the Union Street Inn."

I breathed a sigh of relief. A cooperative suspect. Definitely a good sign.

"Are we still on for the movies?" he asked.

"If your alibi checks out."

We both laughed. He was kidding. I wasn't.

I hung up and called San Francisco.

"Union Street Inn," a woman answered briskly. "Ann Garrity speaking."

"This is Detective Austen of the LAPD," I said, with as much authority as I could muster.

"Really?" she asked, curious. "How can I help you?"

"I'm checking on the whereabouts of one of your guests, a Mr. Cameron Bannick, on the night of February fourteenth."

"Oh, he was here at the Inn."

"Are you sure?"

"Yes, we had a special Valentine's dinner, and I remember seeing him at a table all by himself, and wondering why a handsome man like Mr. Bannick was alone on Valentine's Day."

"So you can say with utter certainty that Cameron Bannick was at your hotel having dinner at 8 P.M. on the fourteenth?"

"Yes, I can."

"Thank you so much."

"My pleasure. May I send you one of our brochures? We have a midweek special, only $89 per night, double occupancy, with complimentary breakfast and afternoon wine bar."

"Sure. Why not?" I gave her my address. Who knew? Maybe some day I'd actually have someone to share a double occupancy with.

I hung up and scooped Prozac into my arms. "Cameron has an alibi, darling! He isn't a murderer, after all!"

Prozac shot me one of her know-it-all looks, as if to say, "Sounds like you've really fallen for this guy."

"I have no idea what you're talking about," I huffed, dumping her unceremoniously on the sofa. "My feelings for Cameron Bannick are strictly platonic. I realize he's undoubtedly gay and couldn't possibly return my affections. Surely you don't think I'd be foolish enough to fall for him, do you?"

She didn't deign to answer this one. We both knew very well just how foolish I was capable of being.

* * *

After my tête-à-tête with Prozac, I decided to pay a visit to the LA Sports Club, hoping to get a chance to talk to Stacy's ex-best friend Iris or Violet or Hyacinth.

I was heading down the path to my car when my neighbor Lance Venable, he of the x-ray hearing, sprang from his front door. Obviously he'd been sitting at his window, just waiting to pounce.

"Oh, Jaine!" he called out.

"Hi, Lance. How's it going?"

Why do I even bother to ask? With Lance, nothing's ever going right.

"Look, I hate to complain. . . ."

No, you don't, I thought. *You love to complain. You majored in complaining at Yenta U.*

". . . But your cat's been pissing on my impatiens again."

It's true. Every once in a while Prozac sneaks out of my apartment for the sole purpose, it seems, of pissing on Lance's impatiens. I think she knows it drives him nuts.

"I'm sorry."

"You should be. There's such a thing as a leash law, you know."

"I think that's for dogs."

"Well, it should be for cats, too." His blond curls shook indignantly. "So the next time you're having one of your heart-to-heart talks with your cat, tell her to quit pissing on my impatiens, okay?"

I swear, the guy must spend his entire life with his ear glued to my wall.

The LA Sports Club is a block-long monument to the Body Beautiful, a Taj Mahal with StairMasters.

All marble and brass and gleaming wood, it's light-years removed from my usual house of exercise, the fungus-infested YMCA.

Most of the members are reed-thin model types who haven't had a hot fudge sundae in decades. (Or if they have, they've promptly barfed it back up.)

Actually, I don't think they let you in if you're bigger than a size twelve. But somehow I managed to suck in my gut and make it past a receptionist with a tony British accent, to the office of Wendy Northrop, Membership Counselor. Or as I came to know her, "Wendy Northrop, Barracuda Saleslady."

Wendy was a haughty brunette, forbiddingly thin. Think Nancy Reagan on diuretics.

"How can I help you?" she said, flashing me a brittle grin.

I could tell by her steely demeanor that she was never going to fall for my phony cop routine, or for my phony reporter routine, so I decided to try the one thing she'd be most likely to fall for: a potential customer.

"I'm thinking of joining your gym."

"Our Club," she corrected me. "We like to think of our guests as members, not customers."

Yeah, right, and I like to think of myself as Julia Roberts.

"Anyhow, I'm thinking of joining."

"Not a moment too soon, lardbucket." Of course, she didn't really say that. But she was thinking it, I know.

"Membership starts at $3,000."

Holy smokes. It was all I could do to keep from sputtering, *You've got to be kidding. Do you realize how many Eskimo Pies I can buy for $3,000?*

Instead I played it cool and said, "Oh?"

"Plus a monthly fee of $300."

There must have been drool seeping out of my slack-jawed mouth because she quickly added, "I realize that's a bit steep for most people."

"No, no, not at all." I tried to look as if I were the kind of person for whom $3,000 was chump change. "It's no problem."

Her smile brightened considerably. "Let me take you on a tour of the facilities. I'm sure you'll be impressed."

Flabbergasted was more like it. Never under one roof had I seen so many big chests, tiny waists, and long manes of lustrous hair. And that's just the guys.

Wendy took me everywhere. The racquetball courts where Type A-Plusses were cheerfully going for each other's jugulars. The Olympic-sized swimming pool where the phrase "swimming with sharks" was undoubtedly coined. The equipment room with StairMasters as far as the eye could see. The plushly carpeted aerobics classes where anorexic women were burning off their last remaining ounces of fat. And the Smoothie Bar where blenders whirred to a disco beat. There was also, unbelievably, a real bar. With actual alcohol. Somehow that didn't quite jibe with the carrot-juice-and-green-tea feel of the place, but I for one liked the idea of kicking back after a grueling workout with a frosty margarita. Which is why I for one have thighs the size of ham hocks.

After a pit stop at the ladies' locker room, where I saw more silicone than Dow Chemical produces in a decade, we headed back to Wendy's office.

"So, what do you think?" she asked when we were sitting across from each other in her all-beige office.

"It's every bit as nice as Stacy told me it would be," I said, carefully piloting the conversation.

"Stacy?"

"Stacy Lawrence," I said solemnly. "The aerobics instructor who was murdered. Poor Stacy was a client of mine."

"A client?"

"I'm an attorney." Good heavens! Would my runaway lying streak never end?

"Really? How interesting."

The dollar signs were now sparkling in Wendy's eyes. She opened her desk drawer and pulled out a contract, confident she had just reeled in a live one.

"Poor Stacy," I said. "I still can't believe she's gone."

Wendy did a very good imitation of someone who actually gave a damn. "I know. It's a tragedy." She shook her head sadly. Then, after a suitable interval of about one millionth of a second, she rallied and asked, "So. Will you be paying for your membership by check or credit card?"

"Stacy was such a wonderful person," I sighed, determined not to be sidetracked.

"Oh, yes," Wendy chimed in, with all the sincerity of a campaign promise. "Stacy was one of the most admired and beloved instructors here at the Club."

As Wendy spoke, I was reminded of the movie *The Manchurian Candidate*, where Frank Sinatra has been brainwashed into saying wonderful things about Laurence Harvey, a guy he really hates. Whenever Sinatra praises Harvey, he speaks in a wooden monotone, a glazed look in his eyes. Wendy had that exact same expression when singing Stacy's praises. I'd have bet my bottom dollar, which was none too far away, that she didn't mean a word of it.

"Of course, you don't have to pay the membership fee in one lump sum. We can break it out in installments if you'd prefer."

"Actually, I'm not sure I'm ready to join right now."

An icy chill descended in the room.

"Oh?"

I rummaged in my purse and pulled out an LA Sports Club ad I'd clipped from *Los Angeles Magazine,* offering a free trial workout to prospective members.

"I think I'd like to try one of these trial workouts first."

"Fine," Wendy chirped, conceding defeat, but only temporarily. "When shall I schedule you? How about Thursday afternoon? We've got Beginner's Stretch at 3 P.M. That should be just right for you."

She obviously had me pegged for the out-of-shape puffball that I was.

"Actually, Stacy often talked to me about another aerobics instructor who worked here. Said she was terrific. I'd really like to be in one of her classes. I can't quite remember her name, though. I think it was Iris or Violet. Some sort of flower name."

"Oh, you must mean Jasmine."

"That's it. Jasmine."

"But Jasmine teaches the advanced workout. That class will be far too strenuous for you."

"Oh, no," I protested. "I'm in much better shape than I look."

Wendy believed that one about as much as I did.

"It meets Thursday at 8 A.M."

"Sounds great. I'll be there."

We exchanged smiley good-byes and I headed out of her office, past the receptionist with the British accent, and into the street, where I was happy to see there were still a few fat people left in the world.

Chapter Eight

On my way back from the gym, I swung by Bentley Gardens, hoping to get a chance to speak with Stacy's neighbors—the Garibaldis and Janet Yoshida.

Luckily, I caught them in. Mr. and Mrs. Garibaldi were exactly as Cameron described them: a frail couple in their eighties who no doubt got winded brushing their teeth. No way could they have bludgeoned Stacy to death. They had trouble enough just answering the door.

I handed them the same line I'd given Daryush, that I was a reporter from *The New York Times*. By now I was beginning to believe it myself. I almost wanted to take out a subscription so I could see my byline on the front page.

"*The New York Times!*" Mrs. Garibaldi cooed. "Imagine that. Your parents must be so proud! Come in. Have a nectarine."

She took me by the elbow and led me into their living room.

"You know Oprah?" Mr. Garibaldi asked.

Mrs. Garibaldi shot him a look. "Now why would she know Oprah?"

"I don't know. She comes from New York. I just thought she might know Oprah."

"Of course she doesn't know Oprah."

"How about Rosie? You know Rosie?"

I assured Mr. Garibaldi that I didn't know Oprah or Rosie. Or Regis. Or Montel. Or Eddie, the dog on *Frasier.* Then I asked them if they'd seen or heard anything suspicious the night of the murder.

"Not a thing," said Mrs. Garibaldi.

"We usually turn down our hearing aids after *Jeopardy,*" Mr. Garibaldi explained.

After promising I'd send them a copy of my story, I thanked the Garibaldis for their time, and their nectarine, and headed down the courtyard to visit Janet Yoshida, the UCLA med student.

Janet was a slip of a thing with a waist the size of my kneecap. She was studying for an anatomy exam when I knocked on the door. Peering out at me from behind thick tortoise-rimmed glasses, she looked about as capable of murder as Mother Teresa. She, too, had seen nothing and heard nothing the night of the murder.

I left her to her textbooks and headed home to get ready for my date with Cameron.

I kept telling myself it was no big deal, just a simple movie date with a platonic acquaintance. Nothing to get into a lather over.

Yeah, right. Four hours later, my bedroom was a shambles. Clothes strewn everywhere. Why was everything so damn tight? One of these days, I really had to switch dry cleaners. They were obviously shrinking my clothes with inferior cleaning fluids.

Finally, after trying on enough clothing to start

my own department store, I decided on the same outfit I'd started off with—a pair of jeans and a T-shirt. I corralled my mop into a ponytail, spritzed myself with Jean Naté, and broke out a pair of suede boots I'd been saving for a special occasion.

Cameron picked me up at seven, his blue eyes crinkling, looking very J. Crew in chinos and a chambray shirt. I found myself wondering how he'd look in something a tad more formal—like a wedding tuxedo.

"What an interesting place you've got," he said, looking around my apartment.

I have to admit, it does have a certain carefree Ikea-ish charm.

"And who's this?" he asked, as Prozac circled his ankles like a lovestruck teenager.

"That's Prozac, my significant other."

"What a doll," he said, scooping her up in his arms.

"She hates strangers," I warned him. "Don't be surprised if she scratches."

Then, before my astonished eyes, Prozac—the same cat who barely acknowledges my existence—started licking Cameron's face with all the abandon of an X-rated movie star. I'm surprised she didn't give him a hickey.

I watched, incredulous, as she lay cuddled in Cameron's arms, licking his face and purring in ecstasy.

God, how I envied her.

Marian's movie was a 1945 RKO musical about two sisters who go to Miami to meet rich husbands. Marian played a hatcheck girl. Not exactly a starring role. But she had a few funny lines, and she knew how to deliver them. The mostly gay audience laughed out loud at her zingers. I could see why Cameron had liked her so much; she looked like she'd be a lot of fun.

Now we were sitting in a coffeehouse called Garland's, in the heart of the distinctly gay district of Silver Lake. The place was loaded with good-looking guys, several of whom had their eyes on Cameron.

Our waitress was a twenty-something sprite with an orange buzz cut and a nose the size of a cherry pit.

"Look at that nose," Cameron whispered. "It's got to be a nose job."

"I don't think so," I said. "Looks to me like she was born with it."

"Okay, I'll ask her," he said, and motioned to her. "Oh, waitress!"

"Cameron, what are you doing? You can't ask someone if she's had a nose job."

"And I don't think those breasts are hers, either."

"You're not going to ask her about them, too?"

"C'mon, this is L.A. She won't mind."

"Hi, guys!" The waitress came bopping up to our table. I was too embarrassed to even look at her.

"Look," Cameron began, "I was wondering . . ."

"Yes?"

"Could we have some refills on our espressos?"

"Sure thing, guys."

She bounced off, and Cameron grinned at me. "Gotcha."

"Oh, you! You really had me going."

And he really did have me going. I couldn't help myself. He was just so darn cute.

"Well, you're sure an easy mark," he was saying to me. "Hope you're not so gullible on the force."

"The force? What force?"

"The police force."

"Oh, right."

He shot me a look.

"You're not really a cop, are you?"

"Oh, fudge. I screwed that one up, didn't I? No, I'm not really a cop."

"I didn't think so."

"What gave me away?"

"Well, for starters," he said, "Elaine told me about your Bloomingdale's press card."

"I should have figured that maybe you two would compare notes."

"And besides, I don't think cops go around saying, 'Oh, fudge.'"

"Yeah, I guess it's not their F-word of choice."

He took a bite of his biscotti. I'd long since finished mine. I'd started out nibbling daintily, hoping Cameron would think I was one of those frail little things who eat like a bird. But somewhere around the fifth nibble, I forgot to be dainty and snarfed them down like a longshoreman.

"Elaine tells me you're a writer."

"Guilty as charged."

"She says you're trying to get this Murdoch guy off the hook."

"I just can't believe he killed Stacy."

"The cops do."

"Cops have been known to make mistakes. Just ask Rodney King."

"Point taken," he said. He still had two biscotti left on his plate. I had to sit on my hands to keep myself from grabbing one.

"But be careful, okay? This detective stuff sounds kind of dangerous."

"I'll be fine. Besides, it's actually sort of exciting. And to be perfectly honest," I said, surprised at my own candor, "I could use a little excitement in my life right now."

He looked up, interested.

"Things a little on the blah side?"

"Terminally."

"Same here."

Really? There was a story behind that remark, one that I was dying to hear.

He picked up one of his biscotti, and then put it down with a sigh. "I've just been through a pretty messy breakup, and I've been spending way too much time staring at the walls."

A breakup. So *that's* why he was alone on Valentine's Day. Who did he break up with, I wondered. A girl? A guy? I had to bite my tongue to keep from asking. And I don't mind telling you I was getting pretty uncomfortable, biting my tongue and sitting on my now-numb hands.

"So," he said, grinning mischievously. "You're looking for excitement. I'm looking for excitement. What should we do about it?"

I had a million ideas, none of which I can repeat in a family murder mystery.

"I know," he said. "Let's go get some margaritas."

Margaritas? What did that mean? Did he want to ply me with tequila so he could take me back to his place and ravish me? Or did he simply want a drink?

Stick around. You'll find out.

Chapter
Nine

We polished off a pitcher of margaritas at a bar down the street. I was hoping Cameron would tell me more about his ex, but we spent the whole time talking about movies. The ones we loved. (*Gone with the Wind. Rosemary's Baby. Shadow of a Doubt.*) And the ones we hated. (*The English Patient. Runaway Bride.* And the complete oeuvre of Pauly Shore.)

Cameron kept his hands to himself and made no romantic moves whatsoever. The whole thing was strictly PG-13.

At 2 A.M., we licked the last of the salt from our margarita glasses, and Cameron drove me back to my place. He insisted on walking me to my door. For a foolish instant, I got excited. He could have just dropped me off at the curb. Did this mean he wanted to ravish me, after all? For the first time in more years than I could remember, I felt stirrings in the vicinity of my G spot.

"This was fun," he said, as we stood at my doorstep.

I stood there tentatively, hoping for a kiss. A hug. Anything involving body contact. But all I got was a crinkly-eyed smile.

"Well, see ya," he said, and started down the path toward his car. As he passed Lance's apartment, I saw Lance at the window, eyeing Cameron with interest.

"Take a number, Lance," I muttered, as I headed off to bed.

I woke up the next morning, bleary-eyed, my head throbbing like an angry rap tune. The first thing I saw when I opened my eyes was Prozac sitting on my chest, demanding to be fed.

As I hauled myself out of bed and staggered into the kitchen, I made a vow: No more margaritas after 11 P.M. Ever. No exceptions. Except maybe if I have them with burritos to absorb the alcohol.

I gave Prozac her breakfast, a smelly can of fish innards optimistically called Shrimp, Cod and Sole Souffle. She pounced on it with gusto, practically inhaling the stuff. You'd think she hadn't eaten for a week.

Trying to ignore the fish fumes, I started to put up some water for coffee. And then suddenly I remembered: My 8 A.M. aerobics class at the LA Sports Club. I looked at the clock: Seven thirty-five.

I tore into my bedroom and threw on a pair of sweats. I'd change into my workout gear at the gym. I grabbed a moldy old leotard that I'd bought for a yoga class at the Y. I'd gone to the class only twice. Unfortunately, I had to drop out to cope with an ever-expanding workload. (Okay, so I dropped out to watch *Seinfeld* reruns.)

I was on my way out the door when the phone rang. I let the machine take it. It was an angry client, wondering whatever happened to the brochure I was supposed to be writing for his company ("E-Mail Etiquette and You"). Just one of several projects I'd been neglecting lately. I vowed to myself I'd work on it as soon as I got back from the aerobics class.

I strapped myself into my Corolla and made my way over to the Sports Club, wishing I'd had time for a cup of coffee and a liposuction. I dreaded having to expose my flab to an aerobics class full of Barbies and Kens.

Miraculously, I made it to the club with five minutes to spare. I showed my Guest Pass to the receptionist with the snooty British accent and girded my loins for the humiliation that was sure to befall me in Advanced Aerobics.

The less said about the whole ordeal the better. I was straining and puffing like I'd never strained and puffed before. And that was just getting my leotards on over my hips.

Jasmine Manning was an exotic beauty with olive skin, startling green eyes, and a waterfall of chestnut curls cascading down her back. It was hard to believe Stacy could have stolen a man away from her.

Jasmine led the class with unbounded energy— part cheerleader, part Marine drill sergeant. My fellow classmates, with their washboard abs and buns of steel, had no trouble keeping up with her. I, on the other hand, with my jello thighs and marshmallow tummy, felt like every breath might possibly be my last. The only parts of my body I managed to move with ease were my eyelids.

Trust me. It was not a pretty picture. My thighs were rubbing together so badly, I was afraid they were going to set my leggings on fire.

But eventually the torture ended, and I hobbled over to Jasmine. I was sweating like a pig, and she was fresh as a daisy, smelling softly of jasmine. How clever of her, I thought, to smell like her name.

"Great class," I managed to gasp.

"Are you all right?" she asked, eyeing me with concern. "Can I get you a glass of water?"

"No, no, I'm fine," I assured her, wondering if I'd ever be able to breathe normally again.

"Are you sure?"

"Yes. I'm fine. Really. But I need to talk to you."

"Sure." She flashed me a bubbly smile. "About what?"

"Stacy Lawrence."

Suddenly the bubbles went flat.

"What about her?"

"You know she was murdered?"

"Yeah," she said, not exactly grief-stricken.

"I need to ask you a few questions."

"Are you from the police?"

"No, I'm an attorney." I liked being an attorney with Wendy, the Barracuda Saleslady, so I thought I'd try it again. "I represent Clive Murdoch."

"Who's that?"

A person I just made up. But, hey. She didn't know that.

"The father of the young man who was arrested for Stacy's murder. Mr. Murdoch believes that his son has been falsely arrested and has hired me to try and find out who committed the crime."

"I'm sorry," she said coolly, "but I really can't help you."

She tossed her curls and turned to go.

"Mr. Murdoch is a very rich man," I called after her. "He's offering a reward of $100,000 for any information leading to the arrest of the real murderer."

She stopped in her tracks.

"Let's go have a smoothie," she said.

The bubbles were back.

Every muscle of my body screeching in protest, I somehow managed to hoist myself onto a stool at the Smoothie Bar. Jasmine slid onto hers like syrup on a stack of pancakes. Throwing calorie caution to the winds, I ordered a thick concoction of bananas, yogurt, and chocolate syrup called a Banana Blast. Jasmine ordered a strawberry smoothie, which she sipped one milligram at a time.

"So," I said, after I'd sucked up half my drink in a single gulp, "tell me about Stacy. Did you like her?"

"Sure. Stacy was great." It was Frank Sinatra in *The Manchurian Candidate* all over again. "I liked her a lot."

"In spite of the fact that she stole your boyfriend?"

Jasmine stirred her smoothie cautiously.

"Who told you that?"

"I have my sources."

"Okay, so I didn't like her. Nobody did. She was an arrogant, self-centered bitch. But that doesn't mean I killed her."

"Of course not. I don't for a minute think you had anything to do with her death," I lied.

Jasmine took a mini-sip of her smoothie, somewhat mollified.

"But just for the record, where were you the night of the murder?"

"If you must know," she sniffed, huffy again, "I was home alone, exfoliating."

"Exfoliating?"

"Leg wax, bikini wax, eyebrow shaping. Once a month I devote an evening to getting rid of unwanted hair."

My mind boggled. If a stunner like Jasmine was home waxing her loins on Valentine's Day, what hope was there for mere mortals like me and Elaine Zimmer?

"Do you have any idea who might have killed Stacy?"

She took a deep breath, clearly reluctant to speak.

"I probably shouldn't be talking to you like this, but I could really use that hundred thousand."

"Go on," I urged.

"Well," she sighed, "it could be Andy."

"Andy?"

"Andy Bruckner. Stacy's boyfriend. My ex."

Ah, the hotshot agent Cameron had told me about. I recognized his name. Andy Bruckner was a major player in Hollywood, a partner at Creative Talent, one of the most powerful agencies in town. CTA represented an impressive roster of directors and writers, the kind of people who earn more money in a year than your average third-world country.

"I think Stacy may have been blackmailing Andy," Jasmine said.

"What makes you say that?"

"It's just a feeling I have. These past few months, Stacy seemed to be buying a lot of expensive things. Diamond earrings. A new stereo. She even bragged that Andy was going to buy her a BMW."

"How do you know Andy didn't give those to her as gifts?"

"Hey, I dated the guy. Andy will spring for dinner and an occasional cashmere sweater. But that's about it. You don't date a guy like Andy Bruckner for gifts."

"What do you date him for?"

All of you out there who think she's about to say "love" or "affection" or "intellectual stimulation," go straight to the back of the class and put on your dunce caps.

"You date him for contacts. Andy knows every producer on every lot in Hollywood."

"But what did Stacy have on Andy to blackmail him with?"

"She probably threatened to tell his wife about their affair."

"Andy's married?"

"Of course. They all are," she said plaintively. "Before Andy was cheating on me with Stacy, he was cheating on his wife with me. Of course, he was still cheating on his wife when he was cheating on me with Stacy. . . ."

Ah, what a tangled web we weave when we're a lecherous agent with a penchant for pretty young things.

"Isn't it possible that Andy might have decided to leave his wife for Stacy? Or that his wife knew about his cheating, and didn't care?"

"No, it's not possible," Jasmine said firmly. "Andy likes to fool around, but he'd never give up his wife."

"Why?"

"Catherine Owens Bruckner is old L.A. money. Tall, cool, beautiful. Very WASPier-than-thou. She's a Jewish-boy-from-Brooklyn's dream come true. The perfect trophy wife. He'd never give her up."

"He wouldn't trade her in for someone younger and firmer?"

"No way. Andy likes being part of Catherine's Old Money world. Besides, the alimony payments would kill him."

"How touching," I said, slurping down the last of my Banana Blast.

"So maybe Andy killed Stacy to shut her up," Jasmine opined.

Maybe, indeed.

"Well, I'd better go," she said, sliding down from her stool. "Or I'll be late for my next class."

"Thanks for all your help, Jasmine."

She gazed at me coolly.

"I can be very helpful for a hundred grand." With a final toss of her curls, she headed back to her torture chamber.

Alone at the bar, I eyed Jasmine's smoothie. She'd barely made a dent in it. I was just about to plunk my straw into its frothy pink foam when I felt someone tap me on my shoulder. I whirled around. It was Jasmine. Yikes, how embarrassing.

"Uh, I hope you don't mind my finishing your smoothie." I blushed. "I thought you were through with it."

"That's okay. Help yourself. I just came back to tell you that Andy is over there." She pointed to a thin, muscular guy standing at the reception desk. Of course, ninety percent of the guys at the Sports Club are thin and muscular. This one had curly brown hair and a decidedly flirtatious manner.

He leaned over and whispered something to the snooty British receptionist. She burst out in a spasm of giggles. "Oh, Mr. Bruckner!" she cooed.

"Later, babe." He shot her a smile that was meant to be devastating and started for the exit.

I regretfully abandoned Jasmine's smoothie and hurried after him.

But just as I reached the exit turnstile, who should pop up in my path but Wendy "The Barracuda" Northrup.

"Ms. Austen!" she said, blocking my exit. "Why don't you come with me to my office, and we can sign those contracts?"

"I'd love to," I lied, "but I'm due in court."

I snaked past her and slipped through the turnstile.

"When can I expect to see you?" she shouted after me.

"When hell freezes over," I muttered under my breath.

I dashed out into the street, just in time to see Andy Bruckner driving away in a black BMW.

Chapter Ten

The first thing I did when I got home from the Sports Club was head for the bathtub.

I don't know about you, but I get some of my best thinking done in the tub. The tub is where I come up with handy euphemisms for my clients' resumes and figure out the answers to stubborn crossword puzzle clues. It's where I make Major Life Decisions, like whether to order Chinese food or pizza for dinner.

The bathtub is where I decided to divorce The Blob. I remember lying there, staring at his shampoo and thinking that I simply could not go on living one more day with a man who washed his hair with Mr. Bubble.

Now I was stretched out in the tub, letting the heat seep into my aching muscles, thinking about Andy Bruckner's black BMW. Didn't Elaine Zimmer say she'd seen a black BMW parked outside Bentley Gardens the night of the murder? Was it possible that Andy was the killer? Had he murdered Stacy to put an end to her blackmail threats, as Jasmine had hinted? Or was Jasmine merely a vengeful bitch, implicating Andy to get even with him for having dumped her?

And what about Jasmine? Maybe she was the killer. Had she really been home, exfoliating, the night of the murder? Or had she been at Stacy's place, bashing her former friend's head with a ThighMaster? Was it a case of hell hath no fury like an aerobics instructor scorned?

I lay there pondering the possibilities and, not incidentally, wondering if I should order Chinese food or pizza for dinner. Finally, when I was as limp as The Blob on our honeymoon, I wrenched myself out of the tub and toweled off.

I thought about going to Andy Bruckner's office at CTA, but then I remembered the phone message from my angry client, the one who was waiting for his brochure. I had to remind myself that, as much fun as I was having in the land of make-believe, I was not actually a reporter. Or a cop. Or an attorney. I was a freelance writer, with bills to pay and a voracious cat to feed.

I slung my hair back into a ponytail, got into my pajamas, and hit the computer.

For the rest of the day, I banged away at "E-Mail Etiquette and You," taking time out only to feed Prozac some Moist Mackerel Morsels and nuke a bag of microwave popcorn for myself.

It was dark out when I finally finished. I read over what I had written, feeling quite proud of myself. Here I'd taken a very boring subject and, in a mere nine hours, turned it into a much less boring subject. If they gave out Pulitzers for corporate brochures, I'd be a sure-fire winner.

It was with great pleasure that I faxed my client my opus. It was with even greater pleasure that I faxed him my invoice.

As if sensing my good mood, Prozac ambled over, rubbing her body against my ankles. It was just her way of saying, "Who cares about your silly brochure? Get your priorities straight. It's time to rub my belly."

I was in the middle of giving Prozac a vigorous belly rub when I realized that, aside from my Banana Blast and microwave popcorn and an old Altoid I'd found next to my keyboard, I hadn't eaten anything all day. Suddenly I was hungry. Too hungry to wait for the pizza delivery guy.

I fixed myself a peanut-butter-and-jelly sandwich and a glass of milk, and hunkered down at my kitchen table with my favorite part of the newspaper—the obituaries.

I don't know why I'm so fascinated with obituaries. I think it was George Burns who once said he read the obituaries every morning just to make sure his name wasn't there. I'm not at that stage of life yet, but I still like to read them. I like reading about women with names like Alma and Gladys who moved out to Los Angeles back when L.A. was still a backwater town. They came here from places like Nebraska and Iowa and married their first husbands, had a bunch of kids, and maybe a job, too, and then the Second World War broke out, and they started working for the Red Cross, and eventually their first husbands died, and they met husband Number Two and possibly Number Three at their bridge clubs, and after their second and third honeymoons, they went back to work, not retiring till at least seventy and not dying till at least eighty-five, leaving a whole passel of loving kids and grandkids and great-grandkids behind.

I read those obits and think to myself, My God, what full lives those women led. And they did it without microwaves or Dustbusters or bikini waxes.

Sometimes when I'm reading about Alma or Gladys, I think about my own life, what gaping holes there are. I ask myself: Do I really want to spend the rest of my life with Prozac as my significant other? Without a husband? Without kids? Without stretch marks? When I die, who'll visit my grave? Whose eyes will mist with tears and remember what a nice person and lousy cook I was?

I tell myself it's The Blob's fault. That he's soured me on men forever. But that isn't true. The truth is I'm a coward. Afraid of taking a chance. Of getting hurt. It's easier to curl up with Prozac and read the obituaries.

And so I sat there that night, scanning the death notices between bites of peanut butter and jelly, looking for long happy lives.

Instead, I found Stacy Lawrence.

There she was, between Morton Landers, Beloved Father and Grandfather, and Frieda Lipman, Cherished Aunt.

If Stacy had been beloved and cherished by anyone, it wasn't mentioned in her obituary. The announcement was short and to the point. Stacy had passed away on the fourteenth. Funeral services would be held on the nineteenth.

The nineteenth was tomorrow, I realized, swallowing a particularly chunky mouthful of peanut butter.

I made up my mind to be there.

Stacy was laid to rest in The Vale of Peace, a sylvan glade dotted with oak trees, floral hedges, and a lovely view of the Hollywood Freeway. The minister conducting the service had to shout to be heard over the roar of the cars whizzing by.

I'd driven over from Beverly Hills and joined the small knot of mourners at Stacy's gravesite, hoping none of them would question my right to be there.

As the minister droned on about how the Lord works in mysterious ways, I studied my fellow mourners.

A middle-aged couple, clearly Stacy's parents, stood at the minister's side, grim and dry-eyed. The woman was an older, faded version of Stacy. She had the hard-bitten look of a truck-stop waitress. I could tell she'd been a beauty once, but those days were a distant memory. Stacy's father was a bloated man with an intricate web of veins on his nose and a gut that threatened to pop his shirt buttons. Neither of them showed any discernible emotion.

Were they struggling to hide their despair? Or was there simply no despair to hide? Was it possible that Stacy's parents weren't all that crazy about their own daughter?

Standing next to Stacy's parents was Daryush Kolchev, the manager of Bentley Gardens. Unlike Stacy's parents, Daryush was full of emotion. Tears misted his raisinette eyes, and periodically he dabbed at them with a none-too-clean hankie.

The other mourners were all young and good-looking. Undoubtedly Stacy's wannabe actor friends. They stood in a semicircle around her grave, dressed trendily in black. I felt like I was at an actor's workshop, and the class assignment had been "Grief." Lots of deep sighs. And downcast looks. Hands demurely crossed. None of it rang true. Except maybe for the guy standing next to me, an ebony-haired hunk with a tasteful gold hoop in one ear. He was crying uncontrollably, tears streaming down his cheeks and glop running from his nose. It wasn't pretty, but I had a feeling those tears were genuine.

The minister went on fighting the roar of the freeway, shouting out nice things about a young woman he probably didn't know.

Somewhere between the eulogy and the Lord's Prayer, I happened to glance over at a nearby oak tree. Standing there, apart from the crowd, was a well-dressed man in a raincoat and sunglasses. I could have sworn I'd seen him someplace before. And I had. It took me a minute or two to figure it out, but then it came to me. It was Andy Bruckner.

What was Andy Bruckner doing at Stacy's funeral? Surely he'd want to try and keep a low profile where Stacy was concerned. Maybe he was crazy in love with her and came to pay his respects. Or maybe he killed her and came to make sure she was really dead.

The possibilities buzzed in my head like flies in an outhouse. This detective stuff was hard work. I was beginning to wonder how Kinsey Millhone ever managed to make it to the letter B, when suddenly the sobbing young man next to me whirled around and shouted, "You killed her!"

He was pointing straight at me.

Everyone was staring at me. I felt like a thug in a police lineup.

"I assure you, I had nothing to do with Ms. Lawrence's death—"

But the hunk didn't hear a word I was saying. Instead, he stormed past me, over to where Andy was standing.

I breathed a sigh of relief. He hadn't been pointing at me, after all. Tears still streaming down his cheeks, he lunged at Andy, shouting, "You sonofabitch! If it weren't for you, Stacy would be alive today!"

I turned to one of my fellow mourners, a pretty young thing with purple hair and a diamond stud in her left nostril.

"Who is that guy?" I asked her.

"Devon MacRae," she said. "Stacy's ex-boyfriend."

Aha. Probably the hunk Cameron had seen with Stacy at the Bentley Gardens swimming pool.

Several of the black-clad actor wannabes now sprang into action and pulled Devon away from Andy. Andy picked up his sunglasses, which had fallen to the ground in the scuffle. He put them on and turned to the rest of us, trying his best to look as if he hadn't been scared out of his wits.

"Drunk," he said dismissively of his attacker.

It was true. I'd gotten a whiff of Devon's breath. There'd been enough gin on it to make a pitcher of martinis.

By now The Vale of Peace security guards had come on the scene and had Devon MacRae in custody.

Very interesting, I thought, as they dragged him away, still screaming curses at Andy. Stacy's ex-boyfriend was a violent man. With a bad temper. And a penchant for booze.

Sure seemed like a hot suspect to me.

Poor Stacy was forgotten in the aftermath of Devon MacRae's outburst. The beautiful young things dropped their mourning poses and huddled together, buzzing about the scene they'd just witnessed.

I walked over to where they were standing.

"Excuse me," I said. "Do any of you know how I can get in touch with Devon MacRae?"

They looked at me coolly. The gal with the purple hair finally piped up. "Last I heard, he was parking cars at Palmetto."

Palmetto—for those of you with better things to do with your life than keep up with Hollywood status symbols—is a mega-trendy L.A. restaurant where the elite meet to bullshit each other over Chinese chicken salads. I made a mental note to stop by and sully their parking lot with my lowly Toyota.

"Thanks," I smiled at my purple-haired friend.

I was just about to turn away when Daryush came bustling over.

"Such a tragedy," he said, taking out his hankie and honking his nose. Now I've never actually heard a duck in heat, but I imagine it would sound a lot like Daryush blowing his nose. A few of the pretty young things looked over at us and giggled.

"And that crazy boyfriend of hers," he sniffled, "making such a scene. Shame on him."

I murmured a sympathetic "hmmm."

"So. You still working on story for *New York Times*?"

"Yes," I nodded, in my most investigative reporter-ish mode.

Daryush turned to the pretty young things. "This lady," he informed them proudly, "is reporter from *New York Times*."

Suddenly, they were all smiles.

All at once, it seemed like everyone was handing

me flyers for upcoming equity-waiver productions. "I'm doing *Hedda Gabler* at the Glendale playhouse," said the girl with the purple hair. "I hope you can make it."

"I'm doing *King Lear* at a Lutheran potluck dinner," said another, thrusting his flyer into my face.

"I'm doing a one-woman show about my life as a salesclerk at The Gap."

Busy little bees, weren't they?

I finally managed to wrench myself away from my new best friends and headed over to the parking lot, Daryush at my side.

"So," I said as we walked along, "I see your wife couldn't make it."

Daryush shifted uncomfortably.

"No. Unfortunately Yetta could not come."

Why did I get the feeling that there'd been no love lost between Yetta and Stacy?

"You be sure and send me your story," Daryush said as he climbed into a dirty white van.

"I will. Don't worry."

I was watching him drive away, wondering if it were at all possible that Yetta had offed Stacy, when I heard a seductive, "Hi, there."

I turned and saw Andy Bruckner, flashing me a high-wattage smile. "I hear you're with *The New York Times.*"

"Uh . . . right."

"And that you're doing a story about Stacy's murder."

I nodded.

"It's a pleasure to meet you, Ms. . . . ?"

I thought about telling him I was Maureen Dowd, but I figured he might actually know the real Maureen Dowd. So I reluctantly went with the truth.

"Austen. Jaine Austen."

And before he could say, "Love your books," I quickly added, "No relation."

"I'm Andy Bruckner of CTA. Perhaps you've heard of my agency."

"Of course, Mr. Bruckner."

"Look, Ms. Austen, I hope you won't misinterpret what happened back there. Devon MacRae is a very unstable young man."

"I could see that."

"I just hope you don't get the wrong idea about Stacy and me. Our relationship was strictly business. Stacy Lawrence was a client of the agency. Nothing more."

I nodded as if I actually believed him.

"So I'd appreciate it if you could keep my name out of your story." He flashed me another smile, half-flirting, half-fawning.

"Sorry, Mr. Bruckner. I can't promise that."

For a fleeting instant, I could see a glint of anger in his eyes. But he quickly blinked it away. "You know," he said, just a little too casually, "we're always looking for new writers at CTA."

"Is that so?"

"You have any movie ideas in that pretty head of yours?"

Good Lord. The guy was about as subtle as a Mack truck.

"Not really."

"Why don't you come to my office, and we'll kick some around? Paramount's looking for romantic comedies. I bet you'd be good at that."

"Really, Mr. Bruckner, I know nothing about making movies."

"That's never stopped anyone before. So how about it. Tomorrow, at four?"

"Okay," I said. "Fine."

"Here's my card."

He handed me his card, with a wink. The same wink he gave to the receptionist at the Sports Club. Then he got in his BMW and drove off.

I realized, of course, that Andy Bruckner had just offered me a whopper of a bribe. If I kept him out of my "story," he'd get me a movie deal. And those movie deals, I knew, could run well into six figures.

I have to admit, I was surprised. Not that he bribed me. After all, this was Hollywood.

No, the surprising thing was that I was actually wondering if I could come up with a movie idea by four o'clock tomorrow.

Chapter Eleven

I drove home, fantasizing all the way.

What if I took Andy up on his offer? What if I came up with a blockbuster movie? Of course, eventually Andy would figure out that I wasn't really with *The New York Times*. But by then, maybe he'd be so in love with my idea that he'd let bygones be bygones and go ahead with the project anyway. Maybe he'd take it to a major studio, and they'd greenlight it at the first pitch meeting, and he'd get me hundreds of thousands of dollars. Maybe even millions.

By the time I pulled up in front of my duplex, I was mentally living at the beach in Malibu, best friends with Babs Streisand, driving a pale blue Jaguar, and married to Mel Gibson.

I was halfway up the path to my apartment, planning my wedding to Mel, when Lance Venable stuck his head out his front door.

"Your phone's been ringing all morning," he said, exasperated.

"That's what telephones usually do," I said, as calmly as I could.

"Can't you turn off the ringer when you're gone? You know how thin the walls are."

The guy was impossible. I'm surprised he didn't cry when I peeled an onion. "Okay," I sighed. "I'll try to remember."

I let myself into my apartment and checked out my answering machine. Two itsy-bitsy messages. That's Lance's idea of ringing off the hook. One was a wrong number, and the other was from Cameron. I got a squishy feeling in the pit of my stomach when I heard his voice on the machine. I tried to tell myself it was just indigestion, but I knew better. I was falling for the guy.

"Hi, Jaine. It's Cameron. You free for dinner tonight? Call me at work. 555-4849."

My heart leapt. He wanted to have dinner. Unlike our trip to see Marian's movie (where I'd paid for my own ticket), this sounded like a real date to me. True, Cameron was probably gay. But I didn't know that for sure. Maybe he was ambivalent about his sexuality. Maybe all it would take to turn the tide was the love of a good woman with a kind heart and generous thighs.

I let myself slide into fantasyland again. Forget Malibu and Mel Gibson. This time, it was me and Cameron honeymooning in Bermuda. There we were on the balcony of our oceanfront hotel suite, the waves lapping gently on the shore beneath us, the balmy night air fragrant with hibiscus or gardenia or whatever it is that blooms in Bermuda. We'd been out all night, dining and dancing under the stars. Now we were back in our five-star suite, alone at last, our bodies aching with desire. And just as Cameron was about to tear off my nightie in a passionate frenzy, my telephone had the nerve to ring.

I whipped it from the receiver angrily. "Yes?" I snapped.

"Ms. Austen, this is Detective Rea, L.A. Police." There was an edge to his voice that I didn't like. "You don't really work for *The New York Times*, do you, Ms. Austen?"

"Well, no."

"Daryush Kolchev seems to be under the impression that you do."

"Really?"

"Apparently you told him you were a reporter with that publication. What's more, you told Wendy Northrop at the Sports Club that you were a lawyer. What next? A medical degree?"

"I was just trying to get some information that might lead to the arrest of the real murderer."

"We've already got the real murderer. And his name is Howard Murdoch."

"I wouldn't be so sure about that. Did you know Andy Bruckner was having an affair with Stacy Lawrence? And she may have been blackmailing him? That sure sounds like a motive for murder to me."

So there, Mr. Smarty Pants!

"Did *you* know," he countered, "that Andy Bruckner has an ironclad alibi for the night of the murder?"

Ooops.

"He was working late in his office, and his assistant was with him the entire time."

Phooey.

"What about a hit man? He could have hired a hit man, couldn't he?"

"Look, Ms. Austen. I've been very patient with

you. But my patience is running out. Leave the detective work to the police. Believe it or not, we know what we're doing."

"Yeah, right. That's why O.J. Simpson is spending the rest of his life playing golf in Florida."

And that's when he hung up on me.

"It was lovely talking to you, too," I said to the dead phone line. *What an unpleasant man*, I thought, as I headed to the kitchen to fix myself some lunch.

Much to my disappointment, a roast-beef sandwich on rye had not miraculously materialized in my refrigerator since the last time I'd looked. I rummaged around in my cupboards and managed to unearth a free sample of cereal that had been left at my front door weeks ago, along with my morning paper. I dug into my Honey Wheat Frosted Sugar Pops with gusto, trying to ignore the fact that I was out of milk and eating them dry.

I stretched out on the sofa, dropping Sugar Pops into my open mouth. Funny, what Detective Rea had said about Andy working late the night of the murder. Why wasn't he home with his wife? After all, the murder had been committed on Valentine's Day, the most romantic day of the year. Was there trouble in the Bruckner household? And did that trouble have anything to do with Stacy Lawrence?

I was just polishing off the last of the Sugar Pops when I remembered Cameron's message.

"Can you believe it?" I said to Prozac, who was napping on top of the bookcase. "An attractive man actually wants to take me to dinner."

Ever the empathetic companion, Prozac yawned and went back to sleep.

I called Cameron's number at the antiques shop.

Now remember, I told myself as the phone rang, *Play it cool. Don't sound too eager. Men like a challenge.*

Cameron answered the phone. "Cameron's."

"Hi, Cameron," I yapped, like an eager puppy. "It's Jaine. I got your message. I'd love to have dinner with you! What a wonderful idea."

Am I hopeless or what?

"That's great."

Then I remembered: I had a class that night at the Shalom Retirement Center.

"But I can't," I sighed. "I've got to teach tonight."

"I didn't know you were a teacher."

"Yes, I teach a memoir-writing class to senior citizens."

"That sounds like a hoot. Can I come?"

"Of course you can come! What a fantastic idea!"

Obviously the concept of "playing it cool" was way beyond my grasp.

Cameron said he'd pick me up, and that we could stop off somewhere for a burger before class. I hung up and did a little happy dance, scaring the bejesus out of Prozac, who stared at me wide-eyed from her perch on top of the bookshelf. I kept it up, dancing on my toes, leaping like a crazed ballerina, until Lance started banging on our shared wall.

"Keep it down in there, willya?"

"No problem!" I sang out.

I had a date with Cameron, and nothing was going to bust my bubble.

Or so I thought.

Cameron picked me up at six. Once again, I'd gone through half my wardrobe trying to decide what to wear. This time, I'd chosen black crepe slacks from Ann Taylor and a luscious ecru silk blouse I'd bought on sale at Nordstrom.

Prozac, the little slut, threw herself at Cameron, rubbing her body against his ankles with such abandon, I was afraid that in three months she'd give birth to a litter of baby ankles. Finally, I lured her away with a can of Tasty Shrimp Entrails. While she was busy slurping up her dinner, I grabbed my class looseleaf binder, and Cameron and I made a break for it.

As we headed down the path to Cameron's car, I could see Lance peeking at us through a slat in his blinds.

Hands off, I thought. *He's mine.*

Cameron's Jeep was a mess. I'd noticed that the night we went out together to see Marian's movie. The backseat was littered with empty water bottles, old invoices, and books of fabric swatches.

It was one of the things I liked about him. Not that I admire sloppiness in a man. I just have this aversion to clean cars after living with The Blob. The Blob had an old British Aston Martin that was the love of his life. He was fanatic about keeping it clean. He kept Windex in his glove compartment, a waste basket dangling from his dashboard, and— you won't believe this—a portable vacuum under his seat. He had a special adapter that allowed him to plug it into the cigarette lighter. Heaven help the poor soul who dropped her gum wrapper on the floor.

So Cameron's Jeep was definitely a welcome change of pace.

I tossed my looseleaf binder into the backseat and climbed in alongside Cameron. I only hoped he didn't notice what a hard time I was having hauling my petite derriere up into the car. Show me a woman who looks graceful getting into a Jeep, and I'll show you a figment of your imagination.

I strapped myself in, taking deep breaths of Cameron's aftershave. It was a lovely citrusy scent, worlds apart from the *eau de sweat* The Blob used to wear.

"So," Cameron said, as we rode over to a nearby In 'n Out Burger. "Anything new on your 'case'?"

"As a matter of fact, I went to Stacy's funeral today."

"You did? What was it like?"

"Dramatic, to say the least."

"Tell me everything!" he said, with the gusto of a dedicated gossip.

And I did. I told him about how Devon attacked Andy. And about the girl with the purple hair, and *King Lear* at the Lutheran potluck dinner, and about Andy trying to bribe me with a script deal.

"Wow," he said when I was through. "I don't believe it."

"What? The part about Devon attacking Andy, or the part about Andy bribing me?"

"No. The part about *King Lear* at the Lutheran potluck dinner."

Then he smiled one of his killer smiles, and I made a mental note, which I mentally underlined several times, *not* to order onions with my burger.

My students buzzed with excitement as I walked into the room with Cameron. The old ladies nudged each other, nodding and smiling. At last, their teacher-who-wasn't-getting-any-younger had found herself a boyfriend. They all beamed like proud grandmas.

Only Mr. Goldman seemed pissed. He snatched up the apple he'd left for me at the head of the table and bit into it so vehemently, I thought he'd lose his dentures.

Good. Let him think I had a boyfriend. Now maybe he'd leave me alone.

I introduced Cameron as my "friend," hoping they'd all think "friend" was a euphemism for "insatiable lover."

He took a seat between Mrs. Pechter ("My son, the plastic surgeon"), and Mrs. Rubin ("My daughter, the psychotherapist"). He flashed them his crinkly-eyed smile, and they smiled back, instantly smitten. Mrs. Rubin, giggling like a schoolgirl, reached in her purse and offered him a mint. Later she'd probably offer him her daughter in matrimony.

I asked who wanted to read first, and Mr. Goldman's hand shot up like a piston. I nodded wearily, and he launched into the latest chapter of his adventures as a carpet salesman. Tonight's installment involved a trip to Las Vegas, where Mr. Goldman had been honored by his peers as Broadloom Salesman of the Year. It also involved his meeting Wayne Newton and Lola Falana, both of whom were performing at his hotel. According to Mr. Goldman, "Lola looked at me with bedroom eyes, and if I wasn't a happily married man, I would've done something about it."

Dream on, Mr. Goldman.

As he went off on a none-too-exciting tangent about the evils of area rugs, I glanced down at my blouse. True to my vow, I hadn't ordered onions with my burger at dinner, but I had ordered ketchup, and now I could see a blotchy red stain on the sleeve. Damn. I couldn't take myself anywhere.

When I looked up, I saw that Mr. Goldman had finally finished.

"Nice work, Mr Goldman," I said, hoping it wasn't obvious to everyone that I hadn't been listening. "Okay, who wants to go next?"

Mrs. Vincenzo raised her hand. I could see Cameron looking at her with interest as she began to read, at her slim dancer's body and her silken hair wrapped in a careless bun at the crown of her head. Mrs. Vincenzo's essay was a wonderful piece about her first job, as a chorus girl at a nightclub in Weehawken, New Jersey.

Cameron sat there, riveted, as she read. I couldn't help thinking about his friendship with Marian Hamilton. How much he seemed to care for her, how much he probably missed her. Maybe he came with me to my class, not for my stimulating company, but simply to find another older woman to take Marian's place.

I barely heard a word anybody read after that; I was too busy thinking about Cameron—and that damn blob of ketchup on my blouse.

When the class finally ground to a halt, Mr. Goldman took me aside.

"Is he your boyfriend?" he asked, jerking his head toward Cameron, who was standing across the room talking to Mrs. Vincenzo.

I thought about lying, but I didn't have the energy.

"No," I said. "He's not my boyfriend."

"I didn't think so," Mr. Goldman said smugly. "He looks like a fairy to me."

"That Mrs. Vincenzo is quite a pistol," Cameron said in the Jeep on the way back to my place.

"Yeah, she sure is," I conceded grudgingly.

"She reminds me of Christine."

"Christine?"

"My ex-fiancée."

My heart lurched hopefully. Clearly Christine had to be someone of the female persuasion. Which meant Mr. Goldman was wrong. And all my suspicions were unfounded. Cameron wasn't gay after all.

"We broke up two months ago."

"How interesting!" I blurted out without thinking. "Not interesting that you broke up with your fiancée. Interesting that you were engaged. I mean, to a woman. I mean . . ." I trailed off feebly.

"You didn't think I was gay, did you?"

"Maybe just a little."

"Don't be embarrassed," he smiled. "It happens all the time. I guess it's one of the occupational hazards of being an antiques dealer."

How nice. A non-homophobic heterosexual. Most guys I know fly into a paranoid dither if you think they might be gay. And heaven help you if you dare to buy them a pink shirt for Christmas.

"No," Cameron said, as we pulled up in front of my apartment. "Christine is definitely a woman. She's a ballerina with the Los Angeles Ballet."

I could just picture her. Some elfin Audrey Hepburn type with long legs and a swanlike neck.

Suddenly, I couldn't decide whether to be glad Cameron wasn't gay, or miserable that I obviously wasn't his type. Face it. Men who like delicate ballet dancers rarely wind up with women who're just inches away from queen-sized panty hose.

"So how come you guys broke up?"

Cameron looked pained.

"She wanted to get married. Unfortunately, not to me."

"I'm sorry."

"Me too."

Then he forced himself to smile.

"So, how about you? You ever been married? Engaged? Or otherwise encumbered?"

"Married. Once."

"And?"

"Not exactly a match made in heaven."

He nodded sympathetically, waiting for me to spill my guts. But I didn't want to bore him with the excruciating details of life with The Blob. (I'm saving that stuff for you.)

And then, before I knew what was happening, he was leaning toward me. For a blissful minute, I thought he was going to kiss me. But all he did was reach into his glove compartment.

"Want a Tic Tac?"

"No, thanks," I said. Then, much too perkily, "Oh, my! Look at the time. I'd better get going."

I reached into the backseat to get my looseleaf binder, my Queen Size fanny jutting out toward Cameron's dashboard. Good Lord. How humiliating. As I struggled to gather some papers that had scattered to the floor, I pictured the headlines: *Giant Ass Attacks Jeep Cherokee, Driver Mistakes It for Inflated Airbag.*

Oh, well. It didn't matter. He was obviously still in love with his ex-girlfriend.

Chapter Twelve

The Creative Talent Agency is in a glitzy high-rise on Sunset Boulevard. The kind of building with wall-to-wall windows and spectacular views. So spectacular that on a clear day, when the fog lifts, you can see the smog.

As I made my way up in the elevator for my meeting with Andy Bruckner, I went over all the movie ideas I'd dreamed up. Which totalled Zero. Nada. Zip. Here was my big chance to become a megabucks screenwriter, and I was blowing it. But somehow, I couldn't bring myself to pitch ideas to a slimebag like Andy.

Instead of dreaming up a high-concept story for Julia or Meg or Cameron, I'd spent the morning working on a mailer for one of my regular clients, Toiletmaster Plumbers ("In a Rush to Flush? Call Toiletmaster!").

I stepped off the elevator onto carpeting so thick, I could barely see my Reeboks. I drifted over to an icy blond receptionist at a brand-new antique desk, reading a paperback copy of Sartre's *No Exit*.

I could see she was on page three. I got the feeling that she'd been on page three for a long time—that page two was a distant memory, and page four an impossible dream. She looked up from her book, and gave me the once-over.

"Delivery?" she asked, looking for a package.

"No," I huffed. "I'm Jaine Austen. I've got an appointment to see Andy Bruckner."

"Yeah, right. And I actually understand this crap I'm reading." Okay, she didn't really say that, but she was thinking it. What she really said was, "Oh?"

She picked up her phone and dialed.

"Hi, Kevin. There's a Ms. Austen here who says she's here to see Andy." She listened to the voice on the other end, then hung up, conceding defeat. "His assistant will be right with you," she said with a grudging smile. "Have a seat."

She gestured to several leather sofas scattered around the room.

I sat down in one of them, across from two lanky guys sporting scruffy jeans and a colorful assortment of nervous tics. Obviously screenwriters. One of them had a script rolled up in his lap and was going over a page of notes; the other tapped his foot in a compulsive staccato on the thick carpeting.

"Can I get you some coffee?" the receptionist asked.

I was just about to say yes, when I saw that she wasn't talking to me. She was talking to the screenwriters.

"No, thanks, hon," the foot-tapper said.

He turned to his partner with a worried look on his face.

"You think maybe we need some comic relief in the decapitation scene?"

I swear, he said that. I'm not making it up. No wonder so many of today's movies look like something unclogged by Toiletmasters.

After a while, a svelte redhead in a suit that cost more than my car came out from an impressive set of double doors and breezed over to the screenwriters. She air-kissed them gingerly, careful not to make body contact, then led them back through the double doors into the inner sanctum.

I sat back and waited. And waited. And waited. People arrived for their appointments, were kept cooling their heels the requisite amount of time, and then were finally ushered through the double doors. I had a mental image of a row of agents, sitting at their desks, playing computer solitaire, counting the minutes till they'd kept their clients waiting long enough.

Most of the clients in the waiting room were writers. I could tell by the scripts in their hands and the paranoia in their eyes. At one point a gorgeous woman with legs that wouldn't quit showed up, and was ushered in right away. She had to have been either an actress or a mistress. One guy showed up in an impressive three-piece suit. I could have sworn he was Ted Turner. But he turned out to be the Xerox repairman.

People came, and people went, and I just sat there. After about forty minutes, I was about to get up and say something to the receptionist when the double doors swung open, and a shorter version of Andy, a curly-haired guy with rolled-up sleeves and Larry King suspenders, came bustling to my side.

"You Jaine Austen?"

"Yes."

"I'm Kevin Delaney, Andy's assistant."

"Nice to meet you."

I held out my hand for a handshake. He stared at it as if it were a cockroach on a bed of basmati rice.

"Sorry," he said curtly, "but your meeting with Andy's been cancelled."

"What?" I said, anger bubbling up from my stomach.

"Andy told me to tell you he knows all about you. He called *The New York Times*. He said he doesn't do business with liars."

"Then I guess he doesn't work much in this town."

"Yeah, right. Biting Hollywood humor. Very funny."

He started back toward the double door.

"Hey! Wait a minute!" I shouted, causing the receptionist to look up, alarmed, from page three of her book.

Mr. Suspenders stopped in his tracks and turned to me.

"Yes?"

"Just when did Andy make this phone call to *The Times*?"

"Yesterday, I think."

"He made me drive all the way over in rush-hour traffic and kept me waiting forty minutes for a meeting he knew he wasn't going to keep?"

"Sure looks that way, doesn't it?" he sneered.

He started to walk away, and I grabbed him by the suspenders.

"Look, you putz," I said, shouting loud enough for all the people in the reception area to hear me, "you tell Mr. Bruckner that I know all about him, too. All about his affair with Stacy Lawrence. And tell him that my next pitch meeting is going to be with the police."

By now, everyone was staring at me. Half of

them, I'm sure, were wondering how they could
work this scene into their next screenplay.

As I stomped over to the elevator, I could hear
the receptionist calling security.

It took a while for an elevator to show up. I
could feel the eyes of the receptionist boring into
my back as I waited.

When the elevator doors finally opened, two
slack-jawed security guards came bounding out.
"Some crazy woman is making a scene at the reception desk," I said, as they hurried past me.
Then I slipped into the elevator and pressed the
"Close Door" button before they discovered that
the crazy woman was me.

I headed down to the garage and picked up my
car from the valet-parking area. A bored cashier
held out her hand.

"That'll be eight dollars, please."

Eight dollars? For a crummy parking spot?

I ground my teeth as I forked over the money.
The cashier smiled and offered me a complimen-
tary chocolate mint. In a wild act of defiance, fu-
eled by my fury at Andy Bruckner, I took two.

I was halfway home, sucking on my four-dollar
mint, when I looked up and saw Palmetto, the
restaurant where Devon MacRae worked parking
cars. On an impulse, I swung into the parking lot.
It was only five o'clock, and the lot was empty.
Three valet parkers were standing at the ticket
booth in their red jackets, shooting the breeze.
One of them was Devon.

The sign at the ticket booth said, "Valet Parking
$4." I'd be damned if I was going to shell out an-
other four bucks. So I swerved into a spot and

parked my car myself. Then I got out and headed over to where Devon was standing with the two other valets, both handsome young Mexican guys.

One of them started to punch me a parking ticket.

"No!" I stopped him. "I'm not going to the restaurant; I'm here to talk to Mr. MacRae."

Devon stared at me blankly, no sign of recognition in his eyes.

"We met the other day at Stacy's funeral," I prompted.

"Oh, right," he said, clearly embarrassed that I'd seen him hauled away by The Vale of Peace security guards.

"Can we talk? In private?"

"Sure."

We walked over to my Corolla. I was trying to decide what profession to assume (lawyer? reporter? police detective?) when Devon made up my mind for me.

"Wait a minute. Now I remember you. You were standing next to me at the gravesite, weren't you?"

"Right."

"You must be the newspaper reporter."

"How did you know?"

"Zane told me."

"Zane?"

"The girl with the purple hair."

"Oh, right. Zane."

"She said you worked for *The New York Times*."

"Mmm," I said, technically not lying.

I halfway expected him to take out a flyer for a play he was starring in. But thankfully, he didn't.

"I hope you won't write about that crazy scene at the cemetery. I don't know what came over me." He shook his head, tears welling in his eyes. "I was just so crazy about Stacy. I guess I went a little nuts."

"Do you really think Andy Bruckner killed her?"

"Who knows?" he shrugged. "I think he's capable of it. Or at least, he's capable of hiring someone to do it."

Aha. So my hit-man theory wasn't so far off base, after all.

"But that's not what I meant when I said if it hadn't been for Andy, Stacy would still be alive today."

"What did you mean?"

"Just that if she hadn't broken up with me, we'd be living together by now, in a place of our own, and she never would have agreed to go out with that lunatic they arrested."

"I'm not so sure that the guy they arrested really killed Stacy. I've interviewed him, and he seems pretty harmless."

"Stacy needed someone to take care of her."

Yeah, right. Like Hells Angels need training wheels.

"Stacy was careless. She didn't watch out for herself. Like that time with the peanut oil."

"Peanut oil?"

"Stacy was allergic to peanuts. Actually, she was allergic to lots of stuff. Peanuts. Strawberries. Pollen. Perfume. But the worst was peanuts. Just one peanut could make her violently ill. Every time she ate out, she had to ask the waiter if the food was cooked in peanut oil. I can't tell you how many times she'd forget to ask.

"Then one night, after she dumped me, she went out with Andy to a Thai restaurant. She forgot to ask about the peanut oil. The next thing you know, she was in the emergency room."

He ran his fingers through his mop of dark hair.

"If she'd been with me, that never would've happened. I would've remembered. They pumped her stomach and kept her in the hospital overnight. Do you think Andy stayed with her? No way. The bum left her there, all by herself, and went running back to his wife. Stacy called me the next day and asked me to come and get her. She asked *me*. Not Andy. Doesn't that mean that I was the one she really loved?"

He looked at me pleadingly, desperate for the answer he wanted to hear.

"Sure," I obliged. "I bet she really did love you."

His eyes shone with gratitude.

"I know this is painful for you, Devon, but aside from Andy, can you think of anybody else who might have killed Stacy?"

"Heck, no. Everybody loved her."

Right. Another keen observer in the Love-Is-Blind Department.

"Anyhow," he said, somewhat uncomfortably, "you're not going to write about what happened yesterday, are you? I'm up for a part in a soap, and I can't afford any bad press right now."

"No, I can honestly say I won't be writing about you in the newspaper."

He grinned an endearing lopsided grin, exposing a mouth full of fabulous caps. With his jet-black hair, luminous brown eyes, and slightly crooked smile, he was an undeniable doll. I doubted he'd be sitting on the shelf for very much longer.

"I guess that's about it," I said. "Thanks for talking with me."

We shook hands, and I got into my car.

"Wow," he said, eyeing the dents in my Corolla, "they sure don't pay much at *The New York Times*, do they?"

I smiled weakly and put my car in gear. As I headed toward the exit, I saw that the lot had started to fill up. The cocktail hour crowd. It was just five-thirty, and already there were three black BMWs parked there.

I turned and saw Devon, waving good-bye.

He seemed like a nice guy. But in the words of that wise old philosopher, Bullwinkle J. Moose, things aren't always what they seem in Frostbite Falls.

It was very possible that Devon MacRae took a black BMW from the Palmetto parking lot, drove over to Stacy's apartment and bludgeoned her to death, then drove back just in time to grin his endearing lopsided grin and pocket a ten-dollar tip.

Chapter Thirteen

Prozac and I were snuggled in bed, going over the facts of the case. Okay, I was going over the facts of the case. Prozac was licking her privates. Some mammals have all the luck.

I'd decided to tackle this whole thing methodically, by jotting down detailed notes on a legal pad. Here's what I jotted:

—*Stacy Lawrence, aerobics instructor and seductress extraordinaire, dumps her boyfriend for a big-time Hollywood agent, and gets her skull bashed in with a Thigh-Master.*

—*Suspects? Scads.*

—*Don't forget to buy Q-Tips. And Oreos.*

Okay, so my mind wandered a little. Clearly, this jotting shtick wasn't working. I tossed my legal pad aside and decided to let my mind wander on its own. I started going over my list of suspects, beginning with my own personal fave—Andy Bruckner.

I remembered what Devon said about Stacy's allergies. About how she almost died at that restaurant with Andy because neither one of them remembered to ask the waiter if the food was cooked in peanut oil. But what if Andy *had* remembered, and kept his mouth shut?

"How's this for a scenario?" I asked Prozac. "Maybe Stacy was beginning to be a problem, threatening to spill the beans to Andy's wife about their affair. So Andy takes her to a Thai restaurant, with plenty of peanut-based dishes on the menu, and conveniently forgets to ask the waiter about peanut oil. Sure enough, she orders a dish cooked in peanut oil and has a violent reaction. Only, unfortunately for Andy, she doesn't die. So he has to take more drastic measures. Like bonking her brains out with a ThighMaster."

I looked over at Prozac for approval. But she just went on licking herself, unimpressed with my powers of deduction.

Then I remembered my hissy fit with Andy's assistant at the Creative Talent Agency. Maybe I shouldn't have threatened to go to the police. If Andy Bruckner had killed Stacy to keep her from blabbing to his wife, what would stop him from killing me?

Suddenly I felt scared. What an idiot I'd been. Why didn't I just pin a bull's-eye to my chest and hand Andy a gun?

I reached out to Prozac, who, sensing I could use a comforting body to curl up with, promptly leapt off the bed and fled to the living room.

I finally managed to calm myself down with a few deep-breathing exercises, and a large glass of chardonnay. After all, I told myself, several people in the waiting room at CTA heard me threaten to go to the police. If I were to turn up dead, Andy would be the first person the cops would question.

Surely Andy wouldn't take that kind of chance. He might be a killer, but he wasn't stupid.

And besides, it was possible that Andy wasn't the killer. It could easily have been Devon. I'd seen his temper in action at the cemetery. He said he'd been crazy about Stacy. Maybe crazy enough to kill her, in one of those if-I-can't-have-her-no-one-else-can fits of passion.

And what about Jasmine Manning? And Yetta Kolchev? Either one of them could have killed Stacy in a jealous rage. And Lord knows how many other women out there had boyfriends or husbands seduced by Stacy. Any one of whom could have flipped out and taken revenge with a ThighMaster.

My brain was overloaded with possibilities, all of them sounding pretty damn plausible. I had plenty of theories. What I didn't have was evidence. Not a shred of the stuff.

I thought about my conversation with Devon MacRae in the parking lot. I had a feeling that he'd said something important, something I should have been focusing on. I sensed that he'd given me an important clue, but for the life of me I couldn't figure out what it was.

Trust me. This detective business is a lot harder than it looks on TV.

I flopped back on my bed, feeling a bit overwhelmed. I was lying there, wondering about the nature of good and evil, and whether or not I had any ice cream in my freezer, when the phone rang.

It was Howard.

"Guess what," he said. "I'm out on bail."

"That's wonderful."

"My mom had to mortgage our house to put up the bond money."

Oh, jeez.

"My attorney says he's pretty sure he can get me off. He's a really nice guy. And very enthusiastic. I'm his first case out of law school."

Double jeez.

"Anyhow, I called to thank you. Detective Rea told my attorney how you came to see him and put in a good word for me. I really appreciate that."

"Believe me, Howard, it was the least I could do."

"You're the only one who came to visit me in jail. Except for my mom, of course."

How utterly pathetic.

"So I'd like to take you to dinner, to thank you."

"You don't have to do that."

"I want to. Really. I thought we could have Chinese food. I know this really nice restaurant on Fairfax. The House of Wonton."

"Sounds great," I lied.

"Meet you there tomorrow at five? I've got an early-bird coupon."

"Terrific," I lied again.

I got off the phone, suffused with pity. Poor Howard. The guy goes out on what probably was the first date of his life and winds up getting arrested for murder. I thought back to what he'd told me, about discovering the body. How he walked into Stacy's dark apartment, confused and concerned, smelling her perfume in the air, and wondering where she was. How he called out to her and, getting no answer, walked down the darkened hallway to her bedroom, only to find her lying there, covered in blood. What a nightmare. And it was all my fault.

I decided to ease my guilt with my good buddies Ben & Jerry.

A half hour later, I was sitting in my kitchen, staring down into an empty carton of Chunky Monkey, when it hit me: the important clue Devon had given me in the parking lot. All evening long it had been buzzing around my brain like an elusive housefly. And now it stood still just long enough for me to figure out what it was.

Devon said Stacy was allergic to lots of things. Peanuts. Pollen. Strawberries. *And perfume!*

Howard said he smelled perfume in the apartment the night of the murder. If Stacy was allergic, the perfume couldn't have been hers. Someone else had to have been in her apartment that night.

And I had a pretty good idea who it was.

I spent the next day putting the finishing touches on my Toiletmasters brochure. A few of my zippier headlines were "Tanks for the Memories" and "Commodes Sure to Bowl You Over." (Hey, I never said I was Shakespeare.)

At about four o'clock, I headed over to the Century City Shopping Mall. Century City used to be part of the back lot at Twentieth Century Fox movie studios. Where Academy Award–winning movies like *The Grapes of Wrath, Gentleman's Agreement,* and *All About Eve* were once made, you can now buy a Gap T-shirt. Inspiring, isn't it?

I was walking past Bloomingdale's, remembering the good old days when I could actually afford to shop there, when who should I see coming toward me but Elaine Zimmer, loaded down with Laura Ashley shopping bags.

"Elaine," I called out. "Hi."

She stared at me blankly.

"Jaine," I prompted. "Jaine Austen."

"Oh, right," she smirked. "How are things at the LAPD? Or *The New York Times?* Or wherever it is you're working this week."

I had the grace to blush.

"Daryush was furious when the cops told him you're not really with *The Times.* Apparently he told his whole family in Russia he was going to be in the paper."

Ouch.

"So how are things going with your 'investigation'?"

"Great," I lied. "And you?" I eyed her shopping bags, bulging with Laura Ashley linens. "On a shopping spree, I see."

"Yes," she beamed. "I'm moving into Stacy's apartment next Saturday." She was about a thousand times chirpier than the last time I'd seen her. "Well, I've got to run. They're having a white sale at Bloomie's."

She waddled off, her shopping bags bouncing at her side. Now that she was about to move into the apartment of her dreams, she was one happy camper.

What a difference a death makes.

As I watched Elaine disappear into Bloomingdale's, I remembered the bloodstains I'd seen in her laundry basket. Was it possible that Elaine killed Stacy to inherit her apartment? Or maybe it wasn't about the apartment. Maybe Elaine killed Stacy simply because she hated her. Maybe Elaine was sick of being a short, stumpy woman no one looked at twice, sick of seeing women like Stacy get everything they wanted in life just because they were beautiful. Maybe she got so fed up with the injustice of it all that she went a little bonkers, like one of her patients in the psychiatric ward.

Lost in thought, I made my way along the mall—past kamakaze shoppers, harried moms, and anorexic fashionistas. I arrived at my destination, a tiny shop that sold "all natural" body oils. I browsed through the fragrances, wondering why on earth anyone would want to smell like "Birch Bark" or "Henna Root."

Finally I found the fragrance I was looking for.

Chapter Fourteen

The House of Wonton is a tiny joint on Fairfax Avenue, sandwiched between a Kosher butcher shop and a used-clothing store.

I showed up for dinner at 5 P.M., while the sun was shining, and most civilized people were still digesting their lunch.

At first I thought the restaurant was empty. But then I saw Howard waving to me from a booth way in the back, next to the kitchen. Poor Howard. The restaurant was deserted, and they still gave him a crummy table. That's the kind of guy he was.

I headed over to join him.

"Hi, Howard," I smiled, sliding into a cracked vinyl banquette.

Howard looked paler and thinner than I remembered him. I guess an all-expenses-paid vacation in the county jail can do that to a guy. His cuticles were practically raw from where he'd been picking at them.

"It's good to see you, Howard."

"You, too." He stared down at his paper place-mat. The man clearly had a thing about making eye contact.

"So how's it going?" I asked.

"Great. Just great. Well, not really. I got fired today."

Oh, God. Poor guy. My guilt count skyrocketed. "Really?"

"My lawyer says we can sue them, just as soon as he gets me off the hook for this murder thing."

"Right."

"Anyhow, I'm really very grateful that you came to visit me in jail. Like I said on the phone, you were the only one who did."

"How about we order some drinks?" I needed one desperately.

"The meal comes with free tea."

"How nice." I smiled weakly. Howard was obviously not a drinker. Or a spender. I flagged down our waiter, a young Asian kid even skinnier than Howard, and ordered a Tsing Tao beer.

"The drinks are on me," I insisted.

"Thanks," Howard said, "but I'll stick with tea."

The waiter shuffled over with a lukewarm beer, which he poured into a piping-hot glass, straight from the dishwasher. As it turns out, that was the highlight of the meal. Howard ordered a Number Sixteen (a glutinous combination plate of chow mein, fried rice, and egg roll). I picked at my Special Ingredient Lo Mein, fairly certain that the special ingredient was rubber cement.

"Don't you like your food?" Howard asked, as I pushed my lo mein around on the plate.

"Oh, no," I said, forcing myself to swallow a mouthful. "It's great."

"Mom and I were just here the other night."

Why did I get the feeling that I was eating their leftovers?

"I guess you and your mom are pretty close, huh?"

"Yeah. She's my best friend. Aside from you, of course."

Oh, God. That one just about broke the needle on my pity-o-meter.

Howard took a sip of tea and sighed deeply.

"I doubt I'll ever get anybody to go out with me now."

"Don't say that, Howard. You're a very nice guy."

"Oh, come on. Dating was bad enough before. But now that I've got an arrest record, it's a joke."

"I'm sure there are plenty of women who'd love to go out with you."

"Oh, yeah? I bet you wouldn't date a guy like me."

"Of course I would."

"How about Saturday night?"

"What?"

Good Lord. Where did *that* come from?

"You said you'd go out with a guy like me," he said, for once looking me straight in the eye. "So I'm asking you out."

"I thought it was a hypothetical question," I stammered. "I didn't think you actually meant me. Specifically."

"I knew it. I told Mom you wouldn't want to go out with me. She told me I had to lower my sights and not keep trying to date unattainably beautiful women. So I thought of you."

Great. In the market for a geek? Call Jaine.

"It's not that I don't want to go out with you, Howard. It's just that . . ."

What? What could I possibly tell him to get rid of him?

". . . I'm engaged to be married."

"You're engaged?"

"Yes," I lied shamelessly.

"Oh."

The look of disappointment on his face was palpable.

"But if I weren't engaged, I'd go out with you. Honest."

"You would?"

"Absolutely," I said, trying with all my might to sound like I meant it.

Howard wanted to believe me, I could tell. He had the same hopeful look in his eyes that I get when the Clinique lady promises me a new lipstick will change my life.

"C'mon," I said. "Let's open our fortune cookies."

Our fortune cookies, baked some time in the Ming Dynasty, had the consistency of dried mortar. I practically needed an ice pick to get mine open.

Howard smoothed out his fortune and read it to me. "You will meet a cute brunette. You will give her money. She is our cashier."

Howard blinked. "That doesn't make sense," he said, looking around. "There's no cashier here."

"I think it's a joke, Howard."

"Oh. Right. Now I get it." He smiled wanly. "So what's your fortune?"

I rummaged through my cookie shards, but my fortune was missing.

Howard looked spooked. "That's bad luck," he said.

I felt a small frisson of fear pricking the hairs at the back of my neck. I told myself I was being crazy. Nothing bad was going to happen to me. Except possibly indigestion from that lousy lo mein.

"Howard, before we go, there's something I want to ask you."

"Sure. Go ahead."

I reached into my purse and pulled out the bottle of body oil I'd bought earlier at the mall.

"Remember how you said you smelled perfume in Stacy's apartment the night of the murder?"

"Yeah."

"Is this what you smelled?"

I handed him the bottle. He opened it and sniffed.

"Yes, this is it."

"Are you sure?"

He nodded solemnly.

"I'll never forget the scent, not as long as I live. What's it called?"

"Jasmine."

I drove home from the Chinese restaurant feeling just like Sherlock Holmes (without the pipe and silly hat, of course). How clever of me, I thought, to remember Jasmine's perfume from my visit to the LA Sports Club. Chances are she'd been in Stacy's apartment the night of the murder. Of course, it could have been someone else smelling of jasmine, but it seemed highly unlikely.

I was so busy congratulating myself on my brilliant powers of observation that at first I didn't see the black BMW parked outside my duplex. By the time I did notice, it was lurching out from the curb in a cloud of carcinogens. Tires squealing and rubber burning, it disappeared down the street before

I could get my brilliant powers of observation to observe the license-plate number.

Once again, I remembered what Elaine had said about a black BMW outside Bentley Gardens the night of the murder. I tried to tell myself that it was just a coincidence. There were a quatrillion black BMWs in the city of Los Angeles, 99.999 percent of them having nothing to do with Stacy's murder. But something in my gut told me that the car I'd just seen was not one of the 99.999 percent.

I hurried up the path to my duplex, half expecting some thug to come leaping out of the azalea bushes. But there was no one in sight—not even Lance, whose apartment was dark.

I let myself into my duplex, and looked around the living room. No bad guys lurking behind the sofa. I searched the apartment for signs of a forced entry, but all the windows were locked. Everything was just the way I'd left it, including Prozac, who was nestled comfortably on my favorite cashmere sweater.

Feeling somewhat reassured, I went to the kitchen and poured myself an inch or five of char-donnay. I gulped it down, and was just beginning to relax, when I glanced down and saw a small white envelope on the living room floor. Someone had pushed it in under the front door. I stared at it for a while, hoping it would go away. Finally I walked over and picked it up, telling myself that it was probably a note from my landlord or Ed McMahon.

The envelope was blank. I opened it gingerly and took out a single sheet of white paper. Cut out in newspaper letters was the warning, "M.Y.O.B." Unless those letters stood for *My Yak is Out on Bail,*

I assumed it meant Mind Your Own Business. A love note, no doubt, from the murderer.

On second glance, I saw that the "B" was pasted onto the paper backwards.

Great. Just what I needed. A dyslexic murderer.

I decided to put the note in a Baggie, to preserve fingerprints, although I suspected that the only fingerprints I'd be preserving were my own. The murderer might have been dyslexic, but he or she was no dummy.

I was scrounging in the cupboard, looking for Baggies, when a piercing scream filled the air. It took me a minute before I realized it was just the phone. I guess it's safe to say my nerves were a tad on edge.

I debated whether or not to let the machine get it, but at the last minute, I picked up.

"Hello?" I said, lowering my voice a decibel, trying to sound like either a guy or a lady with hormone problems.

"Jaine? Is that you?" It was Cameron. "Sounds like you have a cold."

"Oh, Cameron. I'm so glad it's you."

"Why? What's wrong?"

"Oh, nothing. I'm just overreacting."

"To what?"

"It's nothing. Honest."

"Not an acceptable answer. I want to hear about it over dinner."

Yes! He wanted to see me again!

"Actually, I already ate."

"But it's not even seven o'clock."

"I know. I had dinner with Howard Murdoch, a charter member of the Early Bird Dining Club."

"Maybe we can go out for a drink."

"To tell the truth, I'm starving. We ate at a

ghastly Chinese restaurant where flies come to commit suicide. I hardly ate a thing."

"I'll pick you up in a half hour."

I hung up, feeling a lot stronger. I found a Baggie and shoved the dyslexic warning note into the top drawer of my desk, along with a bunch of unpaid bills. I'd be damned if I was going to let it intimidate me.

Cameron took me to a French restaurant on the outskirts of Santa Monica, a cozy place with lace curtains on the windows and wonderful aromas wafting from the kitchen. The owner, a reedy Frenchman with an accent as thick as his leek-and-potato soup, was our waiter. His wife was the chef. And their teenage son was the busboy. It was all so damn sweet.

It was just like Cameron to find such a terrific place. Clearly, the man had great taste. I couldn't help comparing him to my ex-husband, The Blob, whose favorite romantic restaurant had flocked velvet wallpaper and an autographed picture of Ernest Borgnine above the bar.

"So what's happening with your investigation?" Cameron asked, after the owner sat us at a table by the window.

I told him about my trip to Andy's office, my encounters with Devon and Elaine, and my discovery that Jasmine had been in Stacy's apartment the night of the murder. Finally, I told him about the black BMW, and the warning note shoved under my door.

"I don't like it," he said, shaking his head. "That note sounds scary. Maybe you should give this detective stuff a rest."

"I can't."

"Why not?"

"I can't let Howard down. Do you know the poor guy lost his job today?"

"Why can't you let the police handle it?"

"Because they're convinced Howard killed Stacy."

"How can you be so sure he didn't?"

"I just know, that's all."

Cameron shook his head, disapproving. He didn't actually say "tsk tsk," but I know he was thinking it.

"You want my honest opinion, Jaine? I think you're taking a foolish chance. Risking your own safety for someone you don't really know."

He was right, of course. Any sane person would have bowed out of this scenario long ago.

"I know it's weird, but I guess the danger is a turn-on."

"You want danger? Try bungee jumping."

"Honestly, Cameron. For the first time in a long time, I feel energized. And alive."

"Just so long as you stay alive. That's all I'm worried about." He took my hand in his. "This is a *murder* case. Which means you're dealing with a *murderer*. In case you haven't heard, those guys can be dangerous."

When he took my hand, I felt my legs go mushy and my G spot spring into action. Of course, I couldn't tell him that a big part of my newfound *joie de vivre* was having him in my life. So I played it cool and tried not to look as aroused as I felt.

We ate our yummy dinners (trout for me, lamb for him), washed down with a lovely burgundy. Eventually, the owners came out from the kitchen and started eating their meal at a table in the back of the restaurant. A Billie Holiday tape was playing softly in the background. If this had been a movie,

I'd have been Gwyneth Paltrow and Cameron would have been Ben Affleck and by the time dessert rolled around, Ben would have been madly in love with me.

But it wasn't a movie. It was real life. And by the time dessert rolled around, I was feeling the waistband of my jeans digging into my gut.

Cameron insisted on paying for the meal. What with my checkbook balance hovering somewhere in the two-digit neighborhood, I didn't put up much of a protest.

We headed out into the damp night air. I could feel my hair frizzing at the speed of light, but I didn't care. I was *très* mellow from our bottle of burgundy. I hoisted myself up into Cameron's Jeep, giggling, totally unconcerned about how big my fanny looked.

As Cameron made his way onto the freeway, I leaned my head back against the headrest, staring up at the stars through the open moon roof. I was enjoying my lovely wine buzz, humming the theme song to *The Brady Bunch*, when suddenly Cameron cried out, "Shit!"

I sat up with a jolt.

"Some idiot's following us awfully close."

I turned around and saw a car coming at us from behind. It looked for sure like it was going to ram into us.

"Damn it." I could see Cameron's knuckles, white against his skin, as he gripped the steering wheel.

Cameron tried to switch lanes, but the other car swerved out from behind us, cutting us off and trapping us in the left lane. I looked over to see if I could identify the face of the driver. My stomach sank. Whoever was behind the wheel was wearing a ski mask.

I knew then that this wasn't just any ordinary freeway nutcase. I knew then that this was personal.

Cameron kept trying to get out of our lane, but every time he sped up, the masked driver sped up, too, blocking him.

"Jesus," Cameron muttered. "This guy's crazy."

Then suddenly, the other car lurched in front of us and slammed to a stop. I squeezed my eyes shut, certain we were going to plow right into him. But Cameron's reflexes were quick. He jammed on the brakes and swerved onto the shoulder of the freeway, just missing the center divider.

Our attacker took off in a burst of burning rubber.

Extra credit for those of you who guessed:

The car was a black BMW.

Chapter
Fifteen

Cameron and I sat in the Jeep, waiting for our hearts to stop pounding.

"The guy was a maniac," Cameron said, his hands still welded to the steering wheel.

"Or woman. It could have been a woman."

"Whoever it was, that was no random act of violence."

I watched the traffic whizzing past us on the freeway, a steady stream of carefree people who had no idea we'd come *thisclose* to a ghastly pileup.

"Wait a minute," Cameron said, remembering. "Didn't you say the car parked outside your house tonight was a black BMW?"

I nodded solemnly.

"I bet it was the same person. Jaine, I think someone is trying to scare the living daylights out of you."

"Well, it's working."

"I told you this detective stuff was dangerous," he said, gathering his strength and merging the

Jeep back into traffic. "I don't suppose you got the license plate number?"

"No, I was too busy begging God to let us live. Did you?"

He shook his head ruefully. "Do you think we should call the police?"

"What for? They can't do anything without the license plate number."

"I guess you're right. But one thing's for sure. I don't think you should be alone tonight."

"I'll be okay."

"No, really. Why don't you spend the night at my place?"

Needless to say, I didn't need much convincing. Being chased at high speeds by an evil BMW had left me feeling pretty vulnerable. Besides, I didn't feel like going home alone to my apartment for the 4,756th night in a row. For once, I wanted to spend the night with a man, even if it was only platonic.

"If you're sure it's no trouble."

"Of course not."

We stopped at my place to pick up my toothbrush and pajamas, and to check on Prozac. I found her just where I'd left her, napping on my cashmere sweater. Her little pink mouth was open, exposing a gap where some teeth were missing. Lying there like that, mouth open and drooling, she brought back fond memories of The Blob.

I headed for the bedroom, where I grabbed my pajamas and splashed some cologne behind my ears. (Okay, if you must know, in my cleavage, too.)

As Cameron drove us over to his place, I half expected a return visit from the evil BMW. But fortunately, we made it to Bentley Gardens without incident.

Cameron insisted that I take his bedroom.

"I hate putting you out like this," I said.

"Don't worry about it. The couch is really comfortable. Half the time I fall asleep there anyway."

He ushered me into his bedroom, and the first thing I saw was a king-sized bed, swathed in a plush down comforter. I couldn't help wondering if Cameron had been sharing it with anyone lately.

"The bathroom's down the hall. I'll put out some extra towels for you."

"Thanks."

"There's some Excedrin PM in the medicine cabinet if you have trouble sleeping."

"Okay."

"Is there anything else I can get you?"

"Just you, naked on a plush down comforter."

Of course, I didn't say that. I said I was fine, thank you very much, and he said well, good night then, and the next thing I knew I was alone in his bedroom, staring at his king-sized bed. I fought back images of Cameron and his ex-girlfriend writhing around on it, having frantic sex in a tangle of long limbs and flat bellies.

Really, I told myself, I had to stop obsessing about Cameron and his old girlfriend. Instead, I decided to obsess about Cameron and any possible new girlfriends. I scooted over to his closet and checked to see if there were any women's clothes hanging there. Thank goodness there weren't.

I scouted the room for telltale photos of possible lovers, but all I found was a picture of a handsome older couple who I assumed were Cameron's parents.

Having spent at least fifteen minutes snooping, I decided to give it a rest and get into my pajamas. I was halfway undressed when I caught a glimpse of myself in an antique gilt mirror hanging over Cameron's dresser.

Maybe it was the lighting. Maybe it was the wine I'd had at dinner. Or maybe it was being one thin wall away from Cameron. Whatever the reason, I looked sexy. True, my thighs and tush were a tad on the large size, but my waist was small and my boobs still relatively perky. Really, I wasn't bad. I just had to remember to spend the rest of my life lit by a forty-watt bulb.

I suddenly remembered an old movie I'd seen with Robert Montgomery and Carole Lombard. Robert and Carole are staying in a quaint old inn, in separate bedrooms. They're madly attracted to each other. They're both lying in bed, thinking about each other, wishing they were in each other's arms, until finally at the end of the movie, unable to control his raging hormones, Robert throws open the door to Carole's room and climbs in bed with her. Of course, you don't actually see him getting into bed with her because the movie was made back in the forties when that sort of stuff was *verboten,* at least on camera. But you know they're definitely going to be boinking each other that night.

As I put on my pajamas I thought of that movie, wishing that Cameron would be like Robert Montgomery and come bursting through the bedroom door. Just in case, I left the top button of my pajamas unbuttoned.

Then, just as I was climbing into bed, I heard a soft knock on the door.

"Can I come in?"

Who says life isn't like the movies?

"Sure."

I unbuttoned another button on my pajamas.

The door opened, and Cameron popped his head in.

"You want to watch Leno together?"

"Great."

"I'm afraid I've only got one TV, and it's here in the bedroom."

Thank God for single-television households.

"No problem," I said. "I love Leno."

"How about I go make us some cocoa?"

"I love cocoa, too."

I wasn't *too* eager, was I?

He went off to make the cocoa, and I settled down in bed, convinced that this whole cocoa-Leno thing was a prelude to whoopee. We'd be lying together, side by side, bodies practically touching, sensing each other's warmth. We'd both pretend to listen to Jay's monologue, but we wouldn't hear a word he was saying. Then Cameron would make the first move. Gently, he'd pull me toward him, stroking my hair, pulling me closer and closer until finally his lips met mine, and—Good Lord! Where the heck did I think I was, anyway? In some cheesy romance novel?

Suddenly I was scared. Was I crazy, leaping into bed with someone I barely knew?

But that wasn't true, I reminded myself. Technically, this was our third date. Plenty of people go to bed on the third date.

But if we had sex, would he think I was too easy? If we didn't have sex, would he think I was a pill? And most important, if we had sex, would I remember how?

"Jaine? Are you okay?"

Cameron was standing over me, with two mugs of cocoa.

"I'm fine."

"You look sort of funny."

"No, no," I said, buttoning my pajamas clear up to my neck, "I'm fine."

"Well, here's your cocoa."

He climbed onto the bed next to me and switched on the TV. We spent the next hour actually watching Jay Leno. (Well, Cameron was watching; I was too busy wondering when and if Cameron was going to reach over gently, and pull me toward him, closer and closer, etc.) When the show was over, Cameron ruffled my hair, gave me his crinkly-eyed grin, and told me to get a good night's sleep.

Then he walked out into the living room, shutting the door firmly behind him. So much for whoopee.

I lay back on Cameron's bed, smelling the faint scent of his aftershave in the pillows. I couldn't figure out whether I was relieved or disappointed that he hadn't tried anything. A little of both, I decided.

Then I burrowed my head in his pillow and drifted off to sleep.

It was nice waking up the next morning in Cameron's bed. Even if he wasn't in it. I was just happy to be in an apartment with another human being for a change.

I got out of bed and checked myself out in the mirror. The good news: no unsightly sheet wrinkles on my face. The bad news: Somehow in the harsh glare of the morning sun, I'd metamorphosed back into Cinderella's chunky stepsister. Like I said, lighting is everything.

I considered snooping in Cameron's drawers, looking for more clues to his love life, but decided it wasn't worth the risk. Just my luck, he'd come barging in and find me fondling his jock strap. So I curbed my snooping instincts and padded out to the living room, where I found Cameron reading the morning paper, looking rather delicious in shorts and an undershirt.

"Hi," he grinned. "You sleep okay?"

"Great," I said. "How about you?"

"Fine."

"It was awfully nice of you to give up your bed."

"No problem," he said, stretching lazily and giving me a lovely view of his thighs. "What can I get you for breakfast?"

"Oh, no. Let me cook you breakfast. It's the least I can do."

"Okay," he smiled. "Help yourself." He pointed me in the direction of the kitchen. "I've got eggs and bacon and English muffins and oatmeal and bananas." I couldn't help but be impressed. My breakfast menu back home consisted of Cheerios and Pop-Tarts.

"What would you like?" I asked him.

"Surprise me."

I headed for the kitchen, suddenly panicked. Had I lost my mind, offering to actually cook something that couldn't be heated up in the microwave? Oh, well, I told myself, I'd just fry up some eggs. How bad could they be?

As it turned out, astoundingly bad. Think Chernoble.

I just assumed that Cameron's fry pan was

non-stick, but it wasn't, and before I knew it the eggs were permanently bonded to the pan. In a panic I hacked away at them, scraping off as much as I could, and tossing the blackened remains down the garbage disposal.

"How's everything going in there?" Cameron called from the living room.

"Fine, just fine."

At which point, my English muffins popped up out of the toaster, two charred lumps of coal.

I mashed them down the garbage disposal, too.

"By the way, don't use the garbage disposal. It's broken."

Oh, Christ.

Suddenly Cameron was standing there in the doorway. Staring at the clouds of smoke hovering over the kitchen.

"Having trouble?" he asked with a glint of a smile.

"I'm sorry," I confessed. "I burnt the eggs. And the English muffins. And I put them down the garbage disposal."

He sat me down at the kitchen table before I could do any more damage, and then proceeded to whip up bacon and eggs with consummate ease. He was going to make some lucky woman a wonderful wife.

Due to the massive clouds of smoke in the kitchen, we decided to eat our breakfast in the living room. We settled down on the sofa, balancing our plates on our laps.

The bacon and eggs were deelish. At first I tried to peck at them daintily, like a skinny Audrey Hepburnish dancer. But after about three bites, I gave up and wolfed everything down, like a hungry truck driver.

I was just sopping up the last of my eggs with my English muffin when I looked up and saw Cameron watching me intently. Oh, God. What was wrong? Did I have a glob of yolk on my chest?

"I love the way you eat," he said. "With such gusto."

Translation: Gad, what a pig.

"Most women I know just pick at their food. I hate that. Here, finish my bacon."

"I couldn't."

"Go ahead."

"No, really. I'm stuffed. Okay, maybe just a bite."

I popped the bacon in my mouth, and grinned. I couldn't help feeling—in spite of evil BMWs and dyslexic warning notes—that all was right with the world. That all couldn't, in fact, be any righter.

Which was, of course, God's cue to send in the shit. Which She did, right on schedule.

Just as I was finishing the last of Cameron's English muffin, the doorbell rang. Cameron disappeared down the hall to get it. I heard him open the door, and then a woman's voice, soft and sexy.

The next thing I knew, a willowy brunette in tight jeans and a halter top came floating into the room.

I wiped the bacon grease from my mouth, hoping I didn't look as houseboatish as I felt.

"Hey, Jaine," Cameron said, "I'd like you to meet a close friend of mine, Asa Morgen."

I smiled woodenly, wondering just how "close" they were.

"Asa, this is Jaine Austen."

She smiled at me, taking in my pajamas and tousled hair. I could see the look of surprise in her eyes. What, she seemed to be wondering, is Cameron doing with *her*?

As if in answer to her unspoken question, Cameron piped up quickly, "Jaine's a good buddy of mine."

"I knew you couldn't possibly be dating her. Not with those thighs." Okay, she didn't really say that, but I could tell she was thinking it.

"Jaine, Asa is Marian Hamilton's granddaughter."

It was then that I noticed her wedding ring and breathed a sigh of relief. She was married! And, I assumed, out of circulation.

"So nice to meet you," I cooed.

"Can I get you some coffee, Asa?" Cameron asked.

"No, thanks. I just stopped by to give you something." She reached into her bag and pulled out a package wrapped in tissue paper. "Grandma left this to you in her will." Cameron took the package from her hands and gently removed the tissue paper. "It's a picture of her when she was under contract at RKO."

"I always loved this picture," Cameron said. Then he reached over and hugged her. She hugged him back, with just a little too much enthusiasm, if you ask me.

Finally she broke her grip on him and made some noises about having to get to the gym. Cameron walked her to the door.

I picked up the photo of Marian, framed in a lovely silver art deco frame. It was a studio publicity still from the forties. Marian was wearing a two-piece swimsuit and leaning up against a fake palm tree, fake clouds in the sky behind her. Her blond hair sprayed out onto her shoulders, her full lips parted. It was clearly meant to be a sexy pose. But there was something about her, maybe the freckles that weren't quite airbrushed out, or the slightly startled look in her eyes, that made her seem vulnerable and achingly innocent. I could see why Cameron was so fond of the picture.

He came back into the room, grinning.

"How do you like that?" he said. "I bet Asa thought we were having a thing together. Isn't that a hoot?"

I managed to dredge up a weak laugh. I didn't see what was so damned hootworthy about us having a "thing" together.

He picked up the picture of Marian and gazed at it fondly.

"I always wanted this. I'm glad she remembered."

Then he placed it on the mantel of his fireplace. He stood back and admired the effect. "She was quite a woman," he said, his eyes misting over with tears.

Then, clearly embarrassed by his emotions, he made a big show of checking his watch.

"Hey, look at the time. I'd better hurry if I want to open the shop by ten." He started for the kitchen with the breakfast plates. "So, what's on your agenda for today?"

"I think I'll head over to the Sports Club and talk to Jasmine. Maybe I can get her to admit that she was at Stacy's apartment the night of the murder."

Cameron dropped the dishes in the sink with a clatter.

"You're kidding."

"About what?"

"You're not seriously going to do any more detective stuff, are you? Not after what happened last night."

"Of course I am."

"You're nuts. What if the driver in the BMW comes after you again?"

"Don't you see? The whole BMW episode just proves that Howard didn't do it. Someone is trying to scare me. The person who really killed Stacy. And I'm going to find him. Or her."

He shot me a look of disbelief.

"It's just something I have to do," I added feebly.

He walked over and held me by the shoulders. "Jaine, read my lips. What you're doing is dangerous. You could get hurt. Or killed. Maybe even fatally."

He was right, of course. But for some reason, I wasn't afraid. Which just goes to show what a fool I was.

Chapter
Sixteen

Cameron and I got dressed (not together, alas) and headed out of his apartment at about ten. Cameron made me promise to at least consider giving up the investigation. And I did consider it. For all of about three and a half seconds.

We walked along the courtyard, dappled with the morning sun. Birds were chirping, flowers were blooming, and the grass was as lush as AstroTurf. I stopped to look at Stacy's apartment across the way. It was still hard to believe a murder had taken place there.

"I think Stacy's parents are coming this weekend to clear out her stuff," Cameron said, following my gaze.

"Look!" I said.

"Where?"

"The door. It looks like it's open."

I hurried over, and sure enough, the door to Stacy's apartment was open—just a crack.

I peered in, eager to get a glimpse of the murder scene. I have to admit I was surprised at what I saw. I guess I expected the place to be done up in Early Malibu Barbie. With lots of turquoise pillows and conch shells and surfboards propped up against the walls.

But it was actually rather nondescript, decorated with the kind of boring brown tweedy stuff you find at furniture rental places. The living room had no charm, no character. There was only one thing that stuck out like a sore thumb.

And that was Daryush.

He was standing at a desk in the living room, his Pillsbury Doughboy belly threatening to pop the buttons on his workshirt, rifling through the contents of the desk drawers. He shook his head in frustration, muttering in Russian. There was an angry set to his jaw that I'd never seen before.

So intent was he in his search that I probably could have done a tap dance on the kitchen counter and he wouldn't have looked up. But I wasn't taking any chances. I backed away from the door and hurried over to where Cameron was waiting for me at the mailboxes.

"You'll never guess what I just saw."

"The ghost of Stacy Lawrence?"

"No, Daryush."

"Wow, what a surprise. A building manager in the apartment of one of his tenants. Alert the media."

"He was snooping in Stacy's desk."

"Snooping?"

"Yes. As in frantically looking in all the drawers."

"Maybe he was looking for her lease."

"Oh, come on. Even you don't believe that."

"No," he conceded. "I guess I don't."

"Stacy obviously had something Daryush wanted. The question is, did he want it badly enough to kill her?"

"Of course not. Daryush is harmless. The guy can't even kill a cockroach. I should know. I had to pay for my own exterminator."

"He didn't look so harmless to me."

Cameron sighed. "You're not going to give up this detective stuff, are you?"

"I'm afraid not."

"Well, just promise me one thing. If anything goes wrong, if you're in trouble, if you need anything, anything at all . . ."

"Yes?"

"Don't come whining to me."

Of course, he was kidding. At least, I hoped he was.

Cameron dropped me off at my place, and I hurried up the path to my apartment. I opened the front door with some trepidation and found myself staring into a pair of angry green eyes.

Prozac's.

"Where the hell have you been?" she seemed to be saying. Along with "I want my breakfast!" And "I smell bacon on your breath."

I scooped her up in my arms and begged her to forgive me. But she just narrowed her eyes and pouted. And don't tell me cats can't pout. Mine does. Worse than a teenager whose nose ring gets rusty in the rain.

I headed for the kitchen, Prozac skittering around my ankles, and opened a can of Tender Liver & Giblets Souffle.

"Here you go, darling," I cooed. "Breakfast."

Prozac shot me a dirty look.

"Okay, if you want to nitpick—brunch."

While Prozac was busy inhaling her food, I

looked around the apartment. Still no sign of intruders, thank goodness. I checked my answering
machine, wondering if I'd received a phone threat
to go along with my mail threat and freeway threat.
But there was just one benign message. From
Kandi, wanting to know if I was free for dinner
that night. I called her back and set up a time.
Then I called the Sports Club to check on Jasmine's
schedule. Fortunately, she was going to be there all
afternoon.

After a quick shower and a change of outfit, I
once again scooped Prozac into my arms to kiss
her good-bye.

"Forgive me, precious lover doll?"

She yawned in my face, her breath a powerful
melange of liver and giblets.

Some cats really know how to get even.

I was on my way out to the Corolla when I ran
into Lance, who informed me that my refrigerator's motor was awfully loud, and could I please do
something about it.

I ground my teeth to a fine pulp. "Oh, for crying out loud, Lance. I'm sick and tired of your
constant complaints. Put a sock in it, willya?"

Okay, so I didn't really say that. Coward that I
am, I muttered something about reporting the
pesky refrigerator to the landlord and escaped to
my car.

On my way over to the Sports Club, I went over
my growing list of suspects: Andy, Jasmine, Elaine,
Devon, and now Daryush. Just when I thought I
had incriminating evidence against one suspect,
another one cropped up to complicate things.

I found Jasmine drinking mineral water at the
Sports Club smoothie bar. I slipped onto the stool

next to her, eyeing a piece of chocolate cheese-cake in the display case.

"Remember me?" I smiled.

"Sure," Jasmine said, gorging herself on a whole sip of water. "You're Howard Murdoch's attorney. Or a reporter from *The New York Times*. Depending on what day it is."

"I gather you've been talking with Andy Bruckner."

"You gather right."

"Look, I may not be an attorney, or a reporter, but I am investigating this case on behalf of Howard Murdoch."

"Bully for you," she said, and swirled her stool so her back was facing me.

"Can't we please talk?"

"You still offering a $100,000 reward?"

"Afraid not."

"Then we can't talk."

I decided to take a gamble.

"I've got a witness who says he saw you going into Stacy's apartment the night of the murder." (Not true, of course, but she didn't know that.)

She whirled around to face me, fear creeping into her spectacular hazel eyes.

"That's absurd." She tried to fake a laugh.

"He's prepared to sign a sworn statement to that effect."

Her flimsy veneer of bravado crumpled like a Tijuana face-lift.

"Okay, I was at her apartment," she sighed. "I stopped by to pick up a sweater she'd borrowed from me. I'd loaned it to her months ago and she never returned it. So I went over to get it. But she was alive when I left her. Honest."

"One of the neighbors says she heard Stacy arguing with someone."

Was there no end to the lies I was prepared to tell?

"Okay, so we argued. She got a pesto stain on my sweater, and I was pissed. I still am pissed, as a matter of fact. I brought the sweater to my dry cleaners and they're not sure they can get it out."

"You have my deepest sympathies."

"It happens to be cashmere."

Righteously indignant, she grabbed her water and slid off the stool.

"Look, I don't care if you believe me or not. When I left Stacy, she was alive and well and heading for her bedroom to take a nap. I didn't kill her, and I've got nothing to be afraid of."

Then she tossed her mane of dark curls and stomped off.

A very impressive performance. I was sitting there at the smoothie bar wondering whether or not to believe it when a buff young waiter came over and flashed me a blinding smile.

"What can I get you?"

I looked up at the chocolate cheesecake in the display case. Good Lord, after the big breakfast I'd just had, the last thing I needed was a piece of cheesecake.

"Just some mineral water, please."

Okay, so I didn't really say that. I ordered the cheesecake. And I ate it all, every last crumb. Are you happy now?

I was mashing the last of the cheesecake crumbs in the tines of my fork when I felt a sudden chill at my side.

"I'd like a word with you, Ms. Austen."

I turned around to face the stony gaze of Wendy "The Barracuda" Northrop. I popped a smile on my face.

"Oh, hi there, Wendy!"

Wendy didn't bother to smile back.

"I know that you're not really an attorney, Ms. Austen."

"I guess word travels fast in the gym biz."

"We are *not* a gym, Ms. Austen. We are a sports club. One of the country's premiere sports clubs, in fact, and we do not appreciate being lied to."

What was all this "we" stuff? Who did she think she was? Queen Victoria?

"What you did was utterly tacky and underhanded. You really didn't intend to join the club, did you?"

"Not exactly, no."

"Well," she sniffed. "I just want to know one thing."

"Yes."

"Have you changed your mind?"

"Huh?"

"About joining. We're having a half-yearly special. One month of free racquetball for every $3,000 membership."

Incroyable, n'est ce pas? Only in L.A.

"Sounds like quite a bargain," I said, "but I think I'll pass."

Wendy's jaws clamped together in an angry vise.

"In that case, please leave the premises immediately."

"But—"

She pointed to the exit, *très* dramatic.

"Immediately!"

I slunk out the door, a shameless sports club

scofflaw, everyone within earshot of our little scene tsk-tsking in disgust.

I headed over to the parking lot to get my car, still smarting over my public humiliation. But then I saw something that made me forget all about my encounter with The Barracuda. There, in the shadow of his BMW, Andy Bruckner was locked in a steamy embrace with a beautiful young woman. And just who was that beautiful woman?

None other than our gal Jasmine. Now that Stacy was out of the way, it sure looked like she and Andy were an item again. Which kept her firmly entrenched on my list of suspects. According to my lightning calculations, Jasmine had the opportunity for murder. She had a motive.

And who knows? She may even have had the keys to a black BMW.

Chapter Seventeen

"The cockroach was arrested on a morals charge."

Kandi and I were slurping margaritas at our favorite Mexican restaurant, Paco's Tacos, a festive joint with piñatas hanging from the ceiling and burritos to die for.

Kandi was talking about the actor who plays Fred the cockroach on Kandi's show *Beanie & The Cockroach*.

"The guy's insane. He keeps exposing himself to fat ladies. They arrested him in the dressing room at Lane Bryant. Thank God the studio was able to keep it out of the tabloids."

A sweet young Latina in a full skirt and peasant blouse came over to take our orders.

Kandi ordered a shrimp tostada. I was lusting after the beef burrito combination plate, but it had been an astronomically high-calorie day, what with bacon and eggs for breakfast and chocolate cheesecake for lunch. So I decided to keep it light and order the Mexican seafood salad.

"I'll have the beef burrito combination plate." The words flew out of my mouth before I could stop them. "Extra cheese on my refried beans."

I know, I know. I'm impossible. Remind me of this shameful episode the next time I start whining about my big tush.

"Where were you last night?" Kandi asked. "I kept calling, but you weren't in."

"Actually, I spent the night at Cameron's."

"The gay guy?"

"He's not gay."

Kandi's eyes lit up with excitement.

"Does this mean you actually had sex? With another person in the room?"

"No. We haven't slept together."

"Then why were you spending the night at his place?"

"He was afraid I might be in danger."

"From what?"

"It's a long story."

And I told it to her, filling her in on everything that had happened since the last time we talked. I told her about my talk with Devon and my aborted meeting with Andy, about Jasmine's perfume and Elaine's new apartment, and Daryush's habit of going through his tenant's drawers. And, of course, about the evil BMW. All this, while managing to pack away a beef burrito combination plate.

"Good Lord," she said when I was through. "That freeway thing sounds really scary."

"I know I should be frightened, but the crazy thing is, I'm not. Not much, anyway."

"Don't you think you should let the police handle this?"

"I can't. They think Howard did it."

"Of course he did it. That's obvious."

"You don't understand. Howard Murdoch is a shy little nerd. He couldn't possibly have killed anyone."

"Need I remind you that this shy little nerd was found with a bloody ThighMaster in his hands?"

"I don't care. Something in my gut tells me he didn't do it. And I've got to trust my instincts. I'm an excellent judge of character."

"Yeah, right. That's why you wound up marrying The Blob."

She had a point there.

"You've got to promise you'll be careful," she said. "I'm worried about you."

"I promise. I'll be careful."

Kandi licked the last of the salt from her margarita glass.

"So what's with this Cameron guy? You think he's interested in you?"

"Nah. I'm not his type. His last girlfriend had thighs the size of my ankles."

"Oh, well. Who needs him? You're going to meet an absolutely wonderful guy at Christie's."

In all the hoo-ha of the last few days, I'd forgotten about Kandi's scheme to meet Eligibles while bidding for bibelots at an auction house.

"They're having an auction tomorrow. And we're going to be there."

I put up a few feeble objections, but Kandi was firm.

"We're going," she decreed. "Get used to it."

I got used to it, and was just popping the last of my refried beans into my mouth when the waitress came by to ask if we wanted dessert.

They have a marvelous flan on the menu, but

there was no way I was going to order it. No way at all. Not in a million trillion years, I told myself, would I let one more calorie down my gullet.

P.S. It was yummy.

I woke up the next morning consumed with guilt over all I'd consumed the night before. I vowed to go on a strict diet—nothing but veggies and fruit and skinless chicken breasts—a vow that I managed to keep for a full fifteen minutes before I broke down and nuked myself a cinnamon-raisin bagel.

While waiting for the cream cheese to melt on my bagel, I leafed through my Jobs Pending file. Not a pending job in sight. A situation that would normally send me spiraling into a mild case of hysteria. But for some reason, that day I didn't care. Clearly, I was growing more than a little obsessed with Stacy's murder. My mind kept wandering back to the sight of Daryush, standing in Stacy's apartment, going through her desk drawers. What the heck had he been looking for?

I slapped a dab of Smucker's strawberry preserves on top of the melted cream cheese, and reached for the phone.

"Hello, Cameron. It's me. Jaine."

"Hi. How's it going? Have you thought about what I said? About giving up that crazy investigation of yours?"

"Yes, I thought about it."

"And?"

"And I will. Just as soon as we break into Stacy's apartment."

"*What?*"

"Remember what you said about Stacy's parents? How they're supposed to clear out her apartment this weekend? I want to take a look around for clues before they get there."

"Call me nutty, but isn't that the first thing the police do after a murder? Look for clues?"

"Yes, but they look for blood and blunt instruments and stuff like that. We're going to be looking for insignificant stuff the police overlooked. Like, for instance, what Daryush was searching for in Stacy's desk."

"What do you mean, 'we'?"

"I'm going to need your help, Cameron."

"Forget it. I'm not helping you."

"Why not?"

"Ever hear the expression 'breaking and entering'? People get arrested for it all the time."

"Fine," I said, in what I hoped was a tone of icy disapproval, and what I feared was a nasal whine. "If you don't want to help me, I'll manage myself."

There was silence on the line for a few nerve-racking seconds. Then Cameron sighed deeply.

"Okay," he said finally. "I'll help. I'd never forgive myself if something happened to you."

"Oh, Cameron," I squealed. "Thank you, thank you, thank you, you're an angel, an absolute angel—"

"Skip the eulogy, okay? Just how are we supposed to break into Stacy's apartment?"

And I told him my idea.

Chapter
Eighteen

"Mr. Kolchev?" Cameron said into the telephone, lowering his voice a notch or two. "This is Detective Timothy Rea with the LAPD."

I sat across from Cameron on his living room sofa, palms sweaty with anticipation.

"Is he buying it?" I mouthed.

Cameron nodded to me, and went on.

"I'm afraid one of our officers may have left his wallet in Stacy's apartment. It probably fell out of his back pocket when he was dusting for fingerprints in the bedroom. Can you check and see if it's there? It's brown eelskin. The officer's name is Webb. Frank Webb. If you find it, call me: 555-9565 . . . Thanks."

He hung up and grinned. "He bought it."

Cameron was enjoying himself in spite of himself.

We raced to the window and peeked through a slat in the blinds, our eyes trained on Daryush's front door. Sure enough, after a minute or two it opened and Daryush came out, popping what looked like the last of a cheese blintz into his mouth. He wiped his greasy fingers on his T-shirt, then took out his key ring and headed over toward Stacy's apartment.

We waited until he unlocked the door and let himself in.

"Okay, let's go!"

We slipped out into the courtyard and hurried across to Stacy's place. Thankfully, no one was hanging around the pool.

"We're crazy, you know that," Cameron said. "What if we get caught?"

"Oh, come on. What's the worst that can happen?"

"We go to jail for impersonating a police officer. Correction, I go to jail. You stay home and bake me a cake with a file in it."

By now we were at Stacy's front door. Just as we'd gambled, Daryush hadn't closed it behind him. We slipped inside the apartment. We could hear Daryush mumbling to himself as he rustled around in the bedroom. Then we tiptoed to the coat closet and hid inside.

I must say it was rather heavenly, being trapped in a coat closet with Cameron. Standing there huddled next to him in the dark, feeling him so close, breathing in his citrusy aftershave. . . .

Now do you see why I wasn't about to give up this investigation?

Much to my dismay, Daryush didn't linger in the bedroom. Before we knew it, he was stomping across the living room and back out into the courtyard, muttering something about a wild-goose chase. Only with Daryush's accent, it came out "wild-koos chess."

When we were certain we were alone, we ventured

out of the closet, free to explore Stacy's apartment. Everything had gone exactly according to my plan. (If you don't count my heavy breathing in the closet.)

"Hey, look at this " Cameron said. He was standing in front of an oak bookcase. "Who would've guessed Stacy was a reader?"

He pulled out one of the books from the shelves. "*The Complete Guide to Multiple Orgasms.*"

"Oh, brother," I sneered, "what an intellectual." Meanwhile, I made a mental note to log on to Amazon to see if they had any copies.

Cameron walked over to a small desk in the corner of the living room, the desk I'd seen Daryush rifling through.

"Let's see if we can find what Daryush was looking for."

The desk had two drawers, and for the next half hour we went through their contents item by item. But all we found were a bunch of old bills and a pack of Care Free sugarless gum.

"Wait a minute," I said. "I bet there's a hidden compartment somewhere."

Cameron sighed. "Jaine, secret compartments are found in expensive pieces of furniture. I doubt very much we'll find one in a desk made of particle board."

We abandoned the desk, and headed for the bedroom, where we plowed through Stacy's dresser drawers and closets, a search that yielded a treasure trove of crotchless panties and strawberry-flavored vaginal lubricant, but little else.

"I told you, if there was anything here, the police would have found it," Cameron said smugly.

"Okay, okay. You're right. Let's go."

We started for the door, when I stopped and headed back to the bookshelf.

"I'm sorry," I said, sheepishly, "but I can't resist." I took out *The Complete Guide to Multiple Orgasms*. "I've just got to take a look at this."

Cameron grinned.

Like two naughty schoolkids, we opened the book and started to pore over it. And that's when we found the photo. Stuck between pages 156 and 157, smack dab in the middle of the chapter called "The Pros and Cons of Vibrators."

It was a scenic shot of Stacy's bed. Featuring Stacy in a pair of those crotchless panties. And lying there beside her, demonstrating the "pros" of vibrators, was none other than our lovable Russian handyman, Daryush Kolchev.

Cameron whistled softly. "I think we just found what Daryush has been looking for."

I stared at the photo, stunned. And nauseous. The sight of Daryush naked is not a pretty picture.

"My God," I said, "a person could knit a sweater with the hair on that guy's back."

Then suddenly we heard the sound of the key in the lock. We lunged for the hall closet, but it was too late. The door swung open.

And Daryush came storming in.

"What are you two doing here?" he growled.

It was one of those pivotal moments in life, when a person's mettle is tested, and she finds out whether she's got what it takes to come through in a crisis.

Unfortunately, I flunked the mettle test. My first instinct was to make a mad dash for the terrace and hurl myself into the lilac bushes.

But cooler heads prevailed.

Without missing a beat, Cameron said, "I just came to pick up a few of my things."

And with that he pulled *The Complete Guide to Multiple Orgasms* out from where we had jammed it back into the bookshelf.

Daryush stared at him, slack-jawed. "That book belongs to you?"

"Yes," Cameron said, strolling to the bedroom, as innocent as you please. "Be right back," he added with a wink.

Daryush stared at me with glazed eyes. I was expecting him to chew me out for lying to him about being a reporter with *The New York Times*. But that whole episode was forgotten as Daryush stood there, breathing heavily through his mouth, trying to process this latest piece of information. I could practically see the wheels turning in what passed for his brain.

Undoubtedly he was asking himself if Cameron had been having an affair with Stacy. And that question was answered in the affirmative when Cameron came strolling out from the bedroom with the jar of strawberry-flavored vaginal lubricant.

"Well," Cameron said. "I guess that's about it." He took out a key from his pocket and offered it to Daryush. "Would you like my key? I won't be needing it anymore."

Daryush nodded dully, and Cameron tossed him the key.

"I guess we'll be going now." He smiled cordially.

And with that, he took me by the elbow and led me to the front door.

Daryush wasn't the only one who was dazed. Cameron had utterly floored me with his quick thinking and sangfroid. I was crazier about him than ever.

What can I say? I'm a sucker for sangfroid.

"We got away with it!" I whispered, as we hustled across the courtyard back to Cameron's place. "Thanks to you. You were terrific."

"I was, wasn't I?" Cameron preened. "I hate to admit it, but you were right. This detective stuff is fun."

At which point, Daryush stepped out from Stacy's apartment. Cameron, the model tenant, waved to him.

"Bye, now!"

Daryush gave a feeble wave and waddled back to his apartment, a shaken man. He let himself in and disappeared inside, no doubt heading for the kitchen to sedate himself with another blintz or two.

"That key you gave Daryush," I said. "It wasn't really Stacy's, was it?"

"Of course not."

He reached down under a potted azalea at his front door and unearthed a muddy key. "Luckily, I keep a spare."

He wiped off the key with his shirttail and let us in.

"What happens if Daryush tries the key in Stacy's lock, and it doesn't work?" I asked.

"I go to jail, and you bake me that cake with the file in it. Hey, how about I make us some lunch? This life of crime is making me hungry."

"No, seriously," I said, following him as he headed into the kitchen. "What happens if Daryush tries the key?"

"Seriously," he said, taking a can of tuna down from the shelf. "I go to jail. Is tuna okay?"

I must've looked worried because he ruffled my hair and laughed.

"Come on. Daryush won't test the key; that's the last thing on his mind right now. He's too worried about a missing X-rated photo."

I took out the picture of Daryush and Stacy from *The Complete Guide to Multiple Orgasms.*

"What self-respecting Fotomat would develop stuff like that?" Cameron asked as he tossed the tuna into a mixing bowl and spooned in gobs of mayonnaise.

"I still can't get over it," I said. "Stacy and Daryush. Talk about beauty and the beast."

"Who knows? Maybe he's an incredibly studly lover."

"Oh, please. Going to bed with Daryush would be like boffing a hairball."

"Maybe she did it so he'd give her Marian's apartment."

"That's a mighty high price to pay for a terrace," I said, counting the folds in Daryush's belly.

"Do you think it's possible she was blackmailing him?" Cameron mused. "Maybe she threatened to tell Yetta about their affair."

"That's hard to believe. Daryush doesn't look like he's exactly rolling in dough."

"Don't be so sure," Cameron said, spreading the creamy tuna mixture onto slabs of wheat bread. "Rumor has it that he's not just the manager here. Marian once told me that she thought he owned the building."

"Really?"

"Yeah. Marian's theory was that he and Yetta

never told anyone, because it was the perfect excuse not to make repairs. They could always tell tenants that The Landlord said no."

"Then the whole blackmail thing makes sense. If Daryush really does own the building, he's got some major bucks."

Cameron took a tomato out from the fridge and started to slice it.

"Mind if I use your phone?" I asked.

"Sure," he said, artfully arranging the tomato slices onto the tuna. "Who're you calling?"

"The L.A. County Assessor's Office. I want to find out who owns Bentley Gardens."

Having had at least a gazillion clients (okay, three) who lived next to commercial property, I was an ace at writing angry letters complaining about noisy parking lots, loud music, and wheezing air conditioners. I was also an expert at ferreting out elusive property owners. It's easy, really. You just call up the county assessor and give the address, and they tell you who owns the building. It's all a matter of public record, and as a stalwart member of the public, you have a right to know.

So I called the assessor's office and after only about seven centuries on hold, a cheery woman came on the line. I gave her the address of Bentley Gardens, and she told me the name of the owner.

By the time I got back to the kitchen, Cameron had assembled two gloriously thick tuna sandwiches, bursting with tomato and mayonnaise, sliced pickles on the side.

"Well?" Cameron asked. "Is it Daryush?"

"No," I said. "Daryush doesn't own Bentley Gardens."

"Oh."

"His wife does."

"What?" Cameron looked up in surprise from the tuna.

"The owner is Yetta Vlasik Kolchev."

"Very interesting."

"Yep," I said, "Yetta's the one with the bucks in that marriage."

"Which makes Daryush a perfect blackmail victim. 'Cough over some dough,' says the lovely Stacy, 'or I tell your rich wife about our adventures with Mr. Vibrator.' "

Cameron set the two sandwiches down on the table.

"Voila!" he said, with a flourish. "How do they look?"

"Scrumptious. But what're you having?"

"Harty-har. You're a regular little comedian, aren't you?"

(Oh, joy! He called me "little"!)

We dug into our sandwiches with gusto, mayonnaise dribbling down our chins.

"I guess Vlasik must be Yetta's maiden name," I said eventually, coming up for air.

"Maybe she comes from a wealthy family," Cameron suggested.

"Wait a minute. Isn't there a Vlasik auto dealership out in the valley?"

Cameron nodded. "Vlasik BMW."

I was so excited, I almost choked on my pickle slice.

"That means Daryush had access to a BMW! He could be our freeway stalker."

"But how do we know it's the same Vlasik?"

"Easy."

Cameron followed me as I went to the phone

and called information. Two minutes later, I was talking to a bored receptionist at Vlasik BMW.

"Welcome to Vlasik Motors," she intoned, "where customers come first."

"Mr. Vlasik, please," I said, in what I hoped was a passable British accent.

"May I tell him who's calling?" the receptionist asked warily.

"Yes," I said, revving up the accent a notch or two. "Tell him it's Ms. Harrington from Cartier in Beverly Hills."

Cameron rolled his eyes at my theatrics, but it worked. The receptionist put the connection through so quickly, I barely had time to hear the canned spiel about the award-winning service specialists at Vlasik Motors.

Mr. Vlasik came on the line. His thick Russian accent, unlike my British one, was undeniably authentic.

"Ivan Vlasik speaking." (Of course, the way he said it, it came out, "Ivan Vlasik spikking.")

"Mr. Vlasik, I'm calling about the diamond ring you ordered for your daughter Yetta."

"I didn't order a ring for Yetta."

"But I've got the paperwork right here in front of me. I'm just checking on the inscription. 'To Yetta with love from Papa.'"

"You're talking crazy. I never buy retail."

"You do have a daughter named Yetta?"

"Yes. But I didn't buy any ring, and I better not be billed for one."

"Of course not, sir. I'll cancel the order posthaste."

I hung up and grinned triumphantly.

"Yetta's his daughter, all right!"

Cameron shook his head, incredulous.

"*Posthaste?* Where do you think you are? In a P.G. Wodehouse novel?"

"Hey, it worked, didn't it?"

"It sure did," he grinned. "Not that I approve, but you're really pretty good at this detective stuff."

Then he grabbed his car keys and started for the door.

"C'mon," he said. "We'd better hurry if we don't want to get stuck in traffic."

"Where are we going?"

"To do something you should have done a long time ago."

"What?"

"Talk to the police."

Chapter Nineteen

Detective Rea looked up from his desk in annoyance as his assistant ushered us into his office.

"Oh, it's you," he said, with all the charm of an angry rottweiler.

I'd tried convincing Cameron it was a waste of time to go to the cops, but he insisted. He said I wasn't giving Detective Rea a chance, that it was our civic duty to tell him what we knew about the case.

So here we were, sitting across from Detective Timothy Rea, he of the red hair and know-it-all smirk. He sat back in his swivel chair, his hands clasped behind his neck, and gave Cameron the once-over. Probably wondering whose penis was bigger. Rea was that kind of guy.

"I'm a friend of Ms. Austen's," Cameron said. "Cameron Bannick."

Cameron held out his hand. Rea hesitated a beat, then grudgingly reached forward to shake it.

"How can I help you?" he grunted.

"We're here to fill you in on some facts we've discovered about Stacy Lawrence's murder."

"Such as?"

"Such as this."

Cameron handed Rea the picture of Daryush and Stacy cavorting in bed.

Rea snickered like a teenage kid with his first issue of *Playboy.*

"There's no accounting for tastes," he said, tossing the picture back across his desk.

"Detective Rea," I said, trying to keep my annoyance at bay, "Daryush Kolchev was having an affair with Stacy Lawrence."

"Welcome to the club. From what I hear, he was one of many."

"We think she may have been blackmailing him."

Rea took out a rubber ball from his desk drawer and started squeezing it in the palm of his hand—no doubt to prove he had a grip of steel, and to let us know just how bored he was by this conversation.

"Last week, you thought Stacy was blackmailing Andy Bruckner."

"She might have been blackmailing both of them. It's possible, isn't it?"

He looked at me and sighed.

"So what are you saying? That Kolchev killed Stacy? Or was it Bruckner?"

"I don't know. It could've been either of them. Or maybe it was Jasmine Manning. She was at Stacy's apartment the night of the murder. Or Stacy's neighbor Elaine Zimmer. I know it sounds nuts, but she might have killed Stacy to get her apartment. All I know is, there are plenty of suspects out there other than Howard Murdoch."

"Those are very colorful theories, Ms. Austen. I'll have to look into them."

Yeah, right. He'd be looking into them about as fast as I'd be joining the LA Sports Club.

"I think you should know," Cameron said, "that two nights ago Ms. Austen and I were stalked on the freeway."

"Stalked?"

"A black BMW chased us, then cut us off in the fast lane. We almost wound up crashing through the center divider."

"You sure it wasn't just another freeway nutcase?"

"We're sure," Cameron said, a hint of impatience in his voice.

"Did you get the license plate number?"

"No," I said. "It all happened too fast."

"We think someone is trying to get Ms. Austen to stop her investigation of Stacy's murder."

"Not only that, somebody left a warning note at my apartment."

"A warning note?"

"It said M.Y.O.B. Mind Your Own Business. Only the 'B' was backwards. I think the killer may be dyslexic."

"The bottom line," Cameron said, "is that someone is out to intimidate Jaine. Someone who doesn't want her investigating this murder."

Rea thought this over, then sat up straight in his chair.

"I agree with you."

"You do?"

I have to admit I was surprised. Maybe Cameron was right. Maybe I hadn't given Rea a fair chance.

"Someone definitely wants you to stop your investigation, Ms. Austen."

He stopped squeezing his rubber ball and put it on his desk.

"But did it ever occur to you that they're trying to get you to quit nosing around—not because they killed Stacy— but simply because what you're discovering could be embarrassing to them?"

The rubber ball had rolled to the edge of his desk. Now it dropped off onto the floor. Rea ignored it. My guess was he didn't want to bend down in front of us to pick it up. A definite no-no in the world of testosterone power plays.

"Let's say Daryush sent you that note. Let's say he chased you on the freeway. Maybe he just wanted you to butt out so he wouldn't get in trouble with his wife. Same for Andy Bruckner."

I got up from my chair. "Come on, Cameron. I told you this would be a waste of time."

"Look, Ms. Austen. I can't arrest Daryush Kolchev just because he was sleeping with Stacy. If I arrested every guy who slept with Stacy Lawrence, we'd run out of jail cells in no time."

I started for the door.

"Bring me the warning note," he called out. "I'll test it for fingerprints if that will make you happy."

I stopped in my tracks and turned back to him.

"The only thing that would make me happy, Detective, is for you to take me seriously."

And with that I turned and stalked out the door. Which would have been very impressive if I hadn't tripped over that damn rubber ball.

"What a putz," Cameron said, as we headed out to the parking lot. "I felt like taking that ball and bouncing it off his fat head."

"I can't believe I tripped over the damn thing."

"If it's any consolation," Cameron grinned, "you looked very graceful going down."

I blushed at the memory of my humiliation. Landing splat on my tush in front of Cameron and Detective Rea, whom I'm quite certain I saw stifling a laugh.

We'd driven over to police headquarters in Cameron's Jeep. Now, as we headed home on the San Diego Freeway, I have to admit I was a tad paranoid. My heart lurched every time I saw a black BMW, certain it was going to plow right into us. But the trip back home was mercifully uneventful. Just your run-of-the-mill tailgaiters, lane switchers, and bimbos putting on makeup at seventy miles an hour.

"Do you think it's possible Rea was right?" I asked as we pulled up in front of Bentley Gardens. "That our freeway stalker had nothing to do with the murder?"

Cameron thought it over. "I know Rea's a putz, but his theory makes sense."

"Yeah," I admitted grudgingly. "I guess it does."

"Then how come I don't believe it?"

"You don't?"

He shook his head.

"Up to now, I thought Howard was probably the killer. But these past few days have changed my mind. I think there's a killer out there, and it's not Howard."

"Thank goodness," I sighed. "I was beginning to think maybe everybody else was right and I was losing my marbles."

"Nope," he said. "I'm just as nuts as you are."

Then he glanced over at the clock on the dashboard. "Oh, jeez. It's after three."

"Who's taking care of your shop?"

"Actually, no one."

"You mean you shut down your shop just to help me out?"

"Hey, it's slow during the week. No big deal."

But of course it was a big deal. An exceedingly big deal. I felt like throwing my arms around him and giving him a sweet, innocent friendly kiss of gratitude. Oh, who am I kidding? I felt like kissing him for real, hot and sweaty. But I refrained from any lip action, just thanked him again for helping me out. Then I climbed down from the Jeep and walked over to my Corolla.

I'm happy to report that I made it there without landing on my fanny.

"Talk to you later." Cameron waved, then took off down the street. I got in the Corolla, and just as I was buckling my seat belt, I looked down at my T-shirt and discovered a crusty blob of dried-up tuna. It must have landed there while I was eating lunch.

Which meant I'd been walking around all afternoon with tuna on my T-shirt. Good Lord. I can't take myself anywhere.

I headed back home, marveling at the day's events. My head was still reeling at the thought of Daryush and Stacy having sex. I had a hard enough time picturing them in the same species, let alone in the same bed.

And Yetta, Daryush's wife. Who would have thought the frumpy hausfrau buying cubic zirconia from Home Shopping was a wealthy woman?

I pulled up in front of my duplex and made my way up the front path, hurrying past Lance's apartment in case he was lurking, ready to pounce with a new complaint.

I let myself into my apartment and found Prozac right where I left her, napping on my pillow, a trail of kitty litter on the comforter. She leapt off the bed at the sight of me and came bounding to my side like an eager puppy. (No, it wasn't love. It was the tuna on my T-shirt.)

After checking my mail for threatening notes (none) and bills (plenty), I stretched out on the sofa and thought about the case.

Was Daryush the killer?

It could easily have been him stalking us on the freeway. But that still didn't explain the BMW that Elaine saw the night of the murder. Why would Daryush have driven a BMW to Bentley Gardens? He didn't have to drive anything to Bentley Gardens; he already lived there. And if Daryush didn't drive a BMW the night of the murder, who did?

Was it Andy? Or Jasmine? Or had Elaine Zimmer made up the whole story about the BMW to throw suspicion away from herself?

My mind swimming with possibilities, I picked up a pad and pencil and jotted down the following:

My Suspects
by Jaine Austen

ANDY BRUCKNER. Blackmail victim? Killed Stacy to shut her up? Drives black BMW. Says he was at work the time of the murder, but the only one who can back him up is his slimy snake of an assistant, who I wouldn't trust with a ten-foot deal memo.

JASMINE MANNING. Killed Stacy to get her boyfriend back? Admits to being at the scene of the crime. Easy access to black BMW (Andy's). No alibi. No corroborating witnesses. No fat on her inner thighs.

ELAINE ZIMMER. Killed Stacy to get a bigger apartment?

DARYUSH KOLCHEV. Motive same as Bruckner's. Access to BMW. Alibi: Says he was home watching TV with his wife, but he could have slipped out and bonked Stacy to death while his Yetta was in the kitchen fixing him a bowl of borscht.

DEVON MacRAE. Could have killed Stacy in a fit of passion. The old "If I can't have her, no one can" motive. Easy access to BMW at the Palmetto parking lot.

I studied my list. I wish I could say I was struck with a sudden bolt of insight. But sadly, the only conclusion I came to was this:

Practically everybody in L.A. has access to a BMW.

Chapter Twenty

I was curled up in bed with Prozac and my list of suspects, drifting in and out of a delicious nap. It was that wonderful time of the day when the sun is going down and fog is rolling in and you know that at any minute it'll be dark, and you can pour yourself a well-deserved glass of wine.

I was lying there, trying to decide what to defrost for dinner, when the phone rang. It was Kandi.

"You haven't forgotten, have you?"

"No, of course not. Absolutely not. Forgotten what?"

"The auction. Our passport to eligible men. It starts at six."

I looked at my watch. It was twenty of.

"Damn," I said, leaping off the sofa.

"I knew you'd forget. It's all psychological. Deep down, you don't really want to meet anyone."

"Okay, Dr. Freud. Save your insights for Fred the Cockroach. I'll throw on some clothes and get there as soon as I can."

"Throw on something expensive. Rich men are attracted to women who dress well."

"Really? And all along I thought they were attracted to big tits."

I got off the phone and headed to my closet, looking for something that wouldn't get me thrown out of the tony premises of Christie's auction house. I decided on a pair of black slacks, a beige silk blouse, and a houndstooth blazer I'd bought half price at Bloomingdale's.

I hoisted my mop of curls into a ponytail, put on some lipstick, and hurried to the kitchen, practically tripping over Prozac, who, like all cats, labors under the mistaken belief that darting in and around your ankles somehow makes you move faster. Finally, I made it to the kitchen and opened up a can of mystery animal parts optimistically dubbed Gourmet Mixed Grill.

I left Prozac inhaling her dinner and headed off to the auction.

It was rush hour, so traffic was a nightmare. I inched my way over to Christie's, stuck behind an octogenarian going fifteen miles an hour in the left lane. Lewis and Clark made better time than I did.

At last I pulled into one of Beverly Hills' many municipal parking lots and spiraled my way up about a hundred and two levels until I finally found a spot. Too impatient to wait for the elevator, I clattered down a dirty metal staircase, emerging at last onto the pristine streets of Beverly Hills. I dashed down Camden Drive to Christie's, a neo-ritzy ersatz townhouse nestled in the heart of a bunch of latte shoppes.

I came bursting into the lobby, looking very attractive indeed with most of my hair drooping from my ponytail, gasping for air, and a fine mist of sweat on my upper lip. I started across the lobby toward the auction room but was stopped by a band of stunning blond Valkyries who, after looking me up and down with undisguised disapproval, asked me for bank references. They wanted to make sure I had enough money to actually pay for anything I might bid on. After I finished laughing, I explained to them that my bank and I were barely on speaking terms, that my checking account balance was a paltry two-digit affair, and that I was at the auction only as an observer. I promised I wouldn't bid on anything, and reluctantly they let me in.

Looking around the room, I saw that Kandi was right about the auction being filled with attractive wealthy guys. Trouble was, most of them were sitting thighs akimbo with other attractive wealthy guys.

The auctioneer was a tall Brit with a velvet baritone voice. He stood at a podium, next to some more Valkyrie assistants. Another bank of beauties manned a row of telephones, accepting phone bids, most likely from celebrities who didn't want to drive up the prices by appearing in person.

The items for sale were not displayed on the premises as I had imagined they would be, but on a TV monitor next to the auctioneer.

I found Kandi in one of the back rows reading a catalogue, an auction paddle at her side. Thanks to *Beanie & The Cockroach*, her bank account was a lot healthier than mine.

"It's about time," she hissed, as I slid into the seat next to her.

"What did I miss?"

"Not much. The most hideous chair just sold for sixteen thousand dollars."

"I don't want to say anything," I whispered, "but most of these guys look gay."

"Not that one. Over there." She nodded in the direction of a chunky guy across the aisle, in bermuda shorts and a Miami Dolphins baseball cap. Kandi was right. He didn't look gay. He looked like a guy who'd gone out not to bid on collectibles, but for a pastrami on rye.

"Rich but unpretentious," she said, sizing him up.

Just then he looked up at us, and smiled.

"Bingo," Kandi whispered.

We spent the next half hour trying to look as if we were serious buyers. Every once in a while, when she was certain that there were other bidders, Kandi would raise her paddle. Each time she did, I got nervous. What if, God forbid, the other bidders backed out and she was stuck paying sixteen grand for a hideous chair? But, as she whispered to me, she wanted Mr. Pastrami to think she was a player.

Most of the items up for sale were home furnishings from the estates of bygone movie moguls. If you ask me, it was all pretty ghastly, the kind of stuff you see at your elderly aunt's house, who hasn't redecorated since Eisenhower was president. But hey, this was L.A. The stuff was selling for major bucks.

I was sitting there, thinking what fools these Angelinos be, when something popped up on the screen that caught my eye, the first item that I actually would have liked to own.

It was a photo of Cary Grant, in a simple silver frame. The photo had been inscribed, "With Love From Archie." Archie Leach, as I well knew, was Cary Grant's real name. The auctioneer said the frame was a one-of-a-kind piece and had been designed by a famous art deco designer whose name I didn't know. The frame didn't look so one-of-a-kind to me; I'd probably seen knock-off copies of it at K mart.

The bidding started at five thousand. Now I like Cary Grant as much as the next person, but honestly. Five thousand dollars for a picture? Kandi raised her paddle at six. Mr. Pastrami upped the bid to seven. Someone on the phone bid twenty! Twenty thousand dollars for an eight- by-ten glossy. Then, to my horror, I saw Kandi raise her paddle at twenty-five thousand. Oh, jeez, I thought, shifting uncomfortably in my seat, she's going to be stuck this time for sure.

I needn't have worried. Twenty-five thousand dollars was just the beginning. The bids started flying like Frisbees in Santa Monica. The pastrami guy bid thirty, one of the phone people bid sixty, and a frumpy lady in polyester bid seventy-five. Gradually, the other bidders fell by the wayside (Kandi among them, thank goodness). In the end, the frumpy lady in polyester duked it out with one of the anonymous celebs on the phone. The picture finally sold to the phone bidder for one hundred and twenty-three thousand dollars.

Kandi turned to Mr. Pastrami and shrugged philosophically, as if to say, *"C'est la vie."* He flashed her a smile. She flashed him one back.

I was beginning to think that Kandi's crazy let's-meet-guys-at-an-auction scheme was actually working, when out of nowhere a dainty redhead with an impressive set of boobs came gliding down the aisle, a diamond on her wedding-ring finger the size of a grape. She plunked herself down next to Mr. Pastrami and kissed him on his cheek.

Kandi's face fell. "Let's split," she said with a sigh.

The last thing I saw as we headed up the aisle was Mr. Pastrami putting his arm around the redhead's shoulder and copping a feel of one of her impressive breasts.

Score one for the tits.

Kandi turned in her auction paddle to the blondes at the front desk, and we stepped out into the cool night air. We decided to drown our sorrows in burritos, so we headed down Camden to the El Torito Grill, an upscale Mexican joint with plenty of dimly lit booths, just right for girl talk.

"This is insane," Kandi said after two frosty Cuervo margaritas were delivered to our table by our stunning actor/waitperson. "I have a good life. A great job. Lots of friends. Why am I driving myself crazy trying to meet men?"

"Sex?" I hazarded a guess.

"Oh, please. I've had some of my best sex with a Double A battery. I'm beginning to think that Gloria Steinem was right when she said 'A woman needs a man like a fish needs a bicycle.' "

"Did Gloria Steinem say that?"

"Either her, or Ellen DeGeneres. I'm not sure. Anyhow, the point is, I'm sick of this crap. I didn't even think that guy at the auction was cute. He was a tubby dufus that I wouldn't look at twice on the street."

She took a healthy slug of her margarita.

"You've got the right idea, Jaine. From now on, I'm going to be like you. I'm not going to give a shit about guys. If a man comes along, fine, but

I'm not going to run myself ragged chasing after them."

Isn't it ironic? Here Kandi was swearing off men, just when I'd started getting interested in them again.

"From now on I'm declaring a moratorium on men. No more blind dates. No more personals. No more showing up at places just because I think there'll be guys there. No more obsessing. No more plotting. No more—Oh, God. That guy at the bar. I think he's smiling at us."

"Wow. That was some moratorium. Lasted a whole two seconds."

"You're right," she sighed. "Old habits die hard."

"Besides," I said, "I think he's smiling at the twenty-year-old blonde in the next booth."

Kandi turned and saw that there was indeed a young blonde sitting behind us.

"Damn," she said, taking a hefty slug of her margarita. "I'm so sick of blondes, aren't you?"

"Totally."

"Let's move to some place like Malaysia. No blondes there."

"Sounds like a plan."

Our burritos came and we dove into them with gusto. What with Kandi's newfound resolve to give up men, I didn't talk about Cameron and my growing attraction to him. I didn't talk about the murder, either. I guess I wanted a break from thinking about suspects and alibis and bloody Thigh-Masters.

What we talked about mostly was Kandi and why she's so obsessed with meeting men. My theory is that it's an occupational hazard of never having been married. People wonder what's wrong with you. So you want to hook up with someone, any-one, just to prove you're lovable. I think it's one of the reasons I hooked up with The Blob. Either that, or temporary insanity.

After a few hours of soul-searching chatter about life and love and how Jennifer Aniston gets her hair so straight, we finally paid our bill and headed outside. It was ten-thirty, and Beverly Hills was deserted. (After 10 P.M., the only people walk-ing the streets of Beverly Hills are winos, hookers, and ex-New Yorkers.)

We strolled over to where Kandi's car was parked, and hugged each other good-bye.

"Thanks for being my friend," Kandi said, her voice husky with emotion.

"Ditto, kiddo."

"Want me to walk you to your car?" she offered. "Then you can drive me back to mine."

"Nah, that's okay. I'm sure the parking lot's safe."

We hugged each other again, and I headed off to get my car.

The municipal lot was fairly empty at that time of night. My footsteps echoed as I walked past the sleepy attendant on duty at the ticket booth. It sud-denly occurred to me that maybe the lot wasn't so safe after all. I was sorry I hadn't taken Kandi up on her offer. The dimly lit stairwell seemed risky, so I rang for the elevator.

The elevator door opened immediately. I stepped inside and pressed the button for the fourth level. Just as the doors were beginning to shut, a muscu-lar black man dressed in baggy gang-banger shorts came rushing up to the elevator. I prayed the door would shut before he could get on, but he thrust his shoulder inside, and the doors sprang open again.

It was one of those godawful moments when you want to run for your life, but you don't want to seem like a bigoted idiot who assumes every large black man is a thug. I stood there frozen with indecision as the doors slid shut.

"You going to four?" he asked, checking the lit button on the panel.

"Yes."

"Me too."

The elevator creaked its way up to the fourth level. I stood there, cursing myself. I should've run while I had the chance. The elevator finally jerked to a stop, and the doors opened.

I got out. So did the black man in the baggy shorts. I walked over toward my car. Baggy Shorts was right behind me.

I was so busy picturing the possible headlines (*Freelance Writer Mugged in Parking Lot* or *Freelance Writer Strangled With Her Own Control Top Pantyhose*), that at first I didn't hear the roar of the car's engine.

"Hey, lady! Watch out!"

I looked up and saw it coming straight at me. A black BMW. The same black BMW that had come after me on the freeway.

I dived between two parked cars and felt a frightening whoosh of air as the car missed me by inches.

My heart pounding wildly, I watched in horror as the car sped past me down the spiraling path to the exit. But it was going way too fast to negotiate the curve. Brakes screeching, it spun out of control and crashed into a concrete pole, the front end caving in like an expensive Bavarian accordion.

The black man came racing to my side.

"Are you okay?"

"I'm fine," I lied.

Together we walked over to the BMW. At last I'd get to identify my pursuer. I looked in the front seat. Sitting there unconscious, slumped over the steering wheel, was a curly-haired young guy in an Armani suit. At first I had no idea who he was. And then it came to me.

I remembered the day I'd shown up at Andy Bruckner's office, and the obnoxious twerp in the Larry King suspenders who'd given me the brush.

The man behind the wheel—my freeway stalker—was none other than Kevin Delaney, Andy Bruckner's assistant.

Chapter
Twenty-one

The man in the baggy shorts whipped out a cell phone from one of his cargo pockets and called 911. The next thing I knew, Andy Bruckner's assistant was being carted off to the hospital, and I was telling my story to a soft-spoken cop with liquid brown eyes and a sympathetic manner.

I told him how I'd gotten off the elevator, and how the BMW had come charging at me. Baggy Shorts corroborated my story.

"The guy was aiming right for her," he said.

"And it wasn't the first time."

I told the cop how I'd been chased on the freeway, and about the M.Y.O.B. note I'd found on my living room floor. I told him that the driver of the BMW was Andy Bruckner's assistant at CTA, and that Andy had been having an affair with Stacy.

Unlike Rea, this cop actually listened. As I talked, he nodded and took notes. At last, someone was taking me seriously.

When I was through talking, I turned and saw that Baggy Shorts was still at my side.

"You feel okay?" he asked.

"I'm fine," I assured him.

"I'm only asking because I'm a doctor, and you look sort of shaken," he said. "If you need me to be a witness in court, just give me a call." He handed me his card.

"Thanks so much. You've been awfully nice."

"No problem."

Then he got into a Jaguar and drove off. I looked down at his card and saw that my would-be mugger was no ordinary doctor but Chief Cardiovascular Surgeon at UCLA Medical Center. So the next time you need an accurate first impression of someone, don't come running to me.

By now, a tow truck had appeared on the scene, and the BMW was being carted away.

"Can I go now?" I asked the cop.

"Sure. But I'd like to stop by your place and get that note you told me about."

The cop, whose name was Officer Fenton, followed me back to my apartment, which of course made me a nervous wreck. I don't know about you, but I hate driving in front of a cop. I'm certain I'm going to forget to signal or not stop long enough at a stop sign, and that I'll wind up running over a pedestrian that I didn't see because I was too busy looking at the cop in the rearview mirror.

But I'm happy to say we made it back to my place without incident. Nary a pedestrian was harmed. As Officer Fenton walked me up the path to my apartment, I could see Lance peeking out from between his blinds. Apparently the man was surgically attached to his window treatments.

I ushered the cop into my apartment and fished out the M.Y.O.B. note from my desk drawer.

"Here it is," I said, pointing out the "B" pasted on backwards. "I think whoever sent this is probably dyslexic."

The cop nodded. "Makes sense to me."

What a nice guy. Acres nicer than Rea.

He thanked me for my time, and I walked him to the door. As he headed down the path to his squad car, I saw that Lance had left his post at the window and was now standing in his open doorway, in full busybody mode. I quickly retreated back inside, hoping he hadn't seen me.

No such luck. Seconds later he was knocking at my door.

"Jaine," he called out. "Open up."

I'm ashamed to say I spent the next few minutes hiding out in the bathroom until Lance finally gave up and went away.

When I was certain he was gone, I dead-bolted the front door and sank down onto the sofa, exhausted.

Prozac, the little angel, sensing how tired I was, leapt up on my stomach and began yowling for her midnight snack.

"For crying out loud, Prozac, don't you ever lose your appetite?"

She shot me a look as if to say, "Look who's talking."

So I hauled myself up and headed for the kitchen.

"There. I hope you're happy," I said, scooping some gourmet fishguts into her bowl.

Then I staggered to my bedroom, where I fell asleep with my clothes on and slept soundly until 7 A.M. when I was clobbered awake by the insistent ringing of my telephone.

I picked it up groggily.

"Officer Fenton here."

Officer Fenton? Who the heck was Officer Fenton? Then I remembered. The cop with the Bambi eyes.

"Mr. Bruckner's assistant regained consciousness a couple of hours ago. And I thought you might like to know that he's confessed to everything."

I sat up, suddenly wide awake.

"He admits he killed Stacy Lawrence?"

"No. But he does admit he's been stalking you in the BMW. And that he's the one who sent you the warning note. Incidentally, you were right. He is dyslexic.

"He says he was doing everything on orders from Andy Bruckner. He also says that Mr. Bruckner was not, as he claimed, working late the night of the murder. That, on the contrary, he left the office early that evening."

"Sure doesn't look good for Andy, does it?"

"You might want to check out the morning news on TV."

"Thanks. I'll do that."

I hung up and flipped on the television. I zapped back and forth between the local morning news shows, which were filled with hard-hitting coverage of fender benders, smog alerts, and Liz Taylor's latest hip replacement surgery. Finally, after sitting through about twenty minutes of Happy Anchor banter, I found it:

Live footage of the cops escorting Andy into police headquarters. According to the Miss-America-with-a-microphone reporter standing nearby, famed Hollywood agent Andy Bruckner was being arrested for the brutal murder of aerobics instructor Stacy Lawrence.

I watched as Andy cowered behind his $500-an-hour lawyer. He held up his hands to shield his face from the news cameras, and I could see that his Rolex was sharing space on his wrist with an LAPD handcuff.

Nearby, Detective Timothy Rea was talking to reporters, looking as smug as the day I'd first met him. He said he had good reason to believe that Andy Bruckner was responsible for the death of aerobics instructor Stacy Lawrence. I was waiting for him to give me some credit. ("Frankly, we couldn't have solved the case without valuable input from talented freelance writer Jaine Austen.") But all he said was, "No further comment at this time."

Then—just as the camera cut back to the newsroom and a live interview with Liz Taylor's chiropractor—the phone rang. It was Cameron.

"Did you see the morning news?"

"I not only saw it, I'm responsible for it."

"What?"

I gave him an update on last night's adventures in the parking lot and all its ramifications.

He whistled softly.

"So Howard is innocent. We were right all along."

"'We'? What do you mean, 'we'? For the longest time you thought he was guilty."

"Okay, okay. So I came on the bandwagon a little late. Don't I get any credit for being your reluctant Watson?"

"Of course you do," I laughed.

"Seriously, this calls for a celebration. C'mon over to the shop about noon, and I'll take you to lunch."

"Sounds good."

I wrote down the address of his antiques shop

on La Brea Avenue, then padded into the kitchen to brew myself a fresh cup of instant coffee.

I should have been happy, right? After all, I'd helped solve a major murder case. But now that the police had arrested Andy, I wasn't sure they had the right guy.

I know, I'm impossible. Here I'd been bitching and moaning about what a creep Andy was, so you'd think I'd be overjoyed at his arrest. But somehow it didn't feel right to me. As much as I disliked the guy, I couldn't picture him doing the actual killing. He was the kind of person who hired other people to do his dirty work for him.

Was it possible that his assistant Kevin was lying to the cops? Was he the one who bumped off Stacy? Was he a Hollywood barracuda willing to do *anything* to get ahead? Had Andy promised him a promotion? A corner office? A date with Calista Flockhart?

And what about Daryush? I kept thinking about that picture of him in bed with Stacy. He was the kind of guy who stuck his hands down garbage disposals all day. The kind of guy who didn't mind dirty work. I wasn't quite prepared to declare him innocent.

I told myself I was being ridiculous. Surely the LAPD knew what they were doing (if you don't count Rodney King and the Ramparts scandal and the Watts riots). They were trained professionals, right? I'd gotten Howard off the hook, and that was all that mattered.

But then it hit me: Thanks to me, Andy was now *on* the hook. What if he was innocent, too? What if he got convicted on my testimony and spent the rest of his life in jail for a crime he didn't commit? (Notice how I managed to hopscotch effortlessly from one guilt trip to the next in mere seconds. Impressive, isn't it?)

I poured some Folgers Crystals into a cup of boiling water and watched them dissolve. If only everything in life were so easy.

I knew I had to stop fixating on this detective stuff and get back to my real job. Ever since the murder, I'd let my freelance writing gigs slide by the wayside. I had a pile of bills on my desk that were reproducing like rabbits. I needed to think up a clever promotional mailer and drum up some new business. Fast.

I grabbed a pad and sat down at my dining room table to think of ideas. After twenty minutes of brainstorming, the only thing on my pad was Prozac, napping.

My heart just wasn't in it.

You don't have to be Sigmund Freud to figure out what was happening in my tortured psyche. After all the excitement of the past few weeks, the thought of going back to my old life—churning out resumes and Toiletmasters brochures—was more than a tad depressing. Playing detective had been fun. A lot of fun.

And soon, I realized, the thrill would be gone.

Chapter
Twenty-two

I spent the rest of the morning trying to think up ideas for my promotional mailer, but my mind kept drifting back to weightier matters, like what to wear for my lunch with Cameron.

Finally, I gave up and headed for the bathtub, where I soaked for a good twenty minutes. It felt divine. Whatever jangled nerves I had left over from my parking lot adventure the night before were now thoroughly unjangled.

When my muscles were the consistency of over-cooked pasta, I wrenched myself from the tub and toweled off. Then I blow-dried my hair and completed my toilette (or "toilet," as The Blob used to say). My legs could have used a shave, but I didn't bother. No one aside from Prozac and my podiatrist ever looked at them anyway.

Freshly de-frizzed and perfumed, I threw on a pair of jeans, a T-shirt, and an Ann Taylor blazer. Then I tossed Prozac some gourmet mystery meat and headed off for my lunch date with Cameron.

I wasn't two steps out my front door when I was accosted by Lance.

"I knocked on your door last night. How come you didn't answer?"

"I was in the bathroom," I said, which was technically the truth.

"Oh." Lance had the grace to look somewhat embarrassed. But not for long.

"So what were you doing with that cop?" he asked, once again the Grand Inquisitor.

"Having passionate sex on the kitchen floor."

Okay, I didn't really say that. What I said was: "Just once, can't you mind your own business?"

Okay, so I didn't say that, either.

"It's a long story, Lance. I'll explain later."

Then I beat a hasty retreat down the path to my Corolla and threw the car in gear before he could come running after me.

I headed down Olympic Boulevard toward La Brea Avenue, a once seedy but now trendy shopping area.

Cameron's store was tucked into a small lot between a psychic and a vintage-clothing store.

As I walked inside, a buzzer sounded, the kind that lets the shopkeeper know he's got a customer.

Cameron was busy waiting on a Malibu Beach-y woman with streaked hair and stylishly wrinkled linen slacks. He looked up and shot me a smile.

I smiled back and started browsing around, trying my best to look like a paying customer. I was impressed by what I saw. The space was spare and uncluttered; just a few choice pieces of furniture on display. Unlike many "antiques" stores that are really just a step or two above thrift shops, Cameron's place seemed to be stocked with genuine antiques.

(Not that I'd know a genuine antique if it came and sat on my lap, but the stuff looked real to me.)

The Malibu babe was looking at a three thousand dollar chest of drawers.

"I'm thinking of converting it into a hamper," she told Cameron.

A $3,000 hamper! I'm telling you, the people in this town have *way* too much money.

Ms. Malibu seemed a lot more interested in Cameron than she was in the chest. She kept smiling at him in a cutesy way that made me want to grab her fashionably wrinkled linen slacks and give her a wedgie. On closer inspection, I saw that she'd obviously been under the knife a time or two. I was betting that those taut cheeks of hers were probably once her kneecaps. Cameron was friendly but not flirty. After a while, sensing she wasn't getting anywhere with him, she said she'd think about the chest and wandered outside to her waiting Mercedes.

"I thought she'd never leave," Cameron grinned.

"You think she's a serious buyer?"

"Nah. Just killing time between her morning latte and lunch at Spago."

"Your place is terrific," I said. "Such beautiful stuff."

"Wait'll you see what I just got in."

He led me past a curtain to the back of the store, where several pieces of furniture were in various stages of being refinished. He pointed with pride to an intricately carved mahogany bed in the center of the room.

"It's an antique sleigh bed. Isn't it a beauty?"

"Gorgeous," I said, touching the carvings on the headboard.

"But we're not here to talk antiques," Cameron said, going over to a small refrigerator in the corner. "We're here to celebrate."

He reached into the fridge and took out a bottle of champagne.

I looked at the label and blinked in disbelief. "Cristal?" I gasped.

For all you K mart shoppers out there, Cristal is a fancy-dancy champagne that costs about $160 a bottle. I happen to know this for a fact because I've walked past it many a time at my local wine store on my way to the Rotgut Chardonnay section.

"Nothing's too good for my favorite detective," Cameron grinned.

"But that stuff costs a fortune!"

"Don't worry," he assured me. "I can afford it. I made a big sale yesterday. For the first time in a long time, I'm actually able to afford champagne with a cork instead of a screw-top cap. If I could only open the darn thing."

He struggled with the cork until it finally popped out with a whoosh of champagne spray. Quickly, he poured the froth into two coffee mugs.

"Forgive the mugs. I don't usually drink on the job."

He held his coffee mug aloft in a toast. "To Jaine Austen, Defender of the Innocent. Crimefighter Extraordinaire. And Patron Saint of Lost Causes."

The champagne was wonderful. Like velvet with bubbles. I tried not to gulp it down like 7UP.

"I'm proud of you, kiddo," Cameron said. "You stuck by Howard when lesser souls were ready to bail. Because of you, the real murderer will be brought to justice."

I smiled uneasily.

"What? What's wrong?"

"Actually, Cameron, I'm not sure that Andy Bruckner is the murderer."

"You're kidding, right?"

"No. I'm not kidding. I don't think he did it."

"You know what your problem is? You can't take Yes for an answer."

"But—"

"Andy Bruckner is a slime. He was cheating on his wife. He had his assistant out terrorizing you. What makes you think he wouldn't kill somebody?"

"That's just it. He's the kind of guy who has someone *else* do his dirty work. I don't think he'd actually kill someone himself."

"C'mon. He's a Hollywood agent. Those guys make the Mafia look like choirboys."

"But—"

"No more buts. I mean it. This is a celebration, and that's what we're going to do. Celebrate."

And then Cameron did the most amazing thing. He put down his mug and kissed me. For real. On the lips. Mouth open. A little tongue. A soft, sweet, gentle kiss that aroused the hell out of me.

"I've been wanting to do that for the longest time," he said when we finally broke apart.

"You have?" I was beyond stunned. "I didn't think you were interested in me that way."

"And I didn't think *you* were interested in *me*."

"But I was," I confessed.

"Remember that night when I drove you home from your class, and you bent over to the backseat to get your books? It was all I could do to keep my hands off you. You've got one terrific tush, you know that?"

Then he started kissing me again, and before I

knew it, we were rolling around on that antique sleigh bed like two crazed teenagers.

No doubt about it. I had died and gone to heaven.

Then suddenly we heard the front door buzz open.

"Damn," Cameron hissed. "A customer."

He got up from the bed and peeked out from behind the curtain.

"It's a decorator," he whispered to me, "a really important client."

"Hi, Marilyn," he called out, tucking his shirt back in his slacks. "Be with you in a minute."

"Cameron, honey," a raspy cigarette voice called back. "Great news. I'm decorating a house in Bel Air. Six thousand square feet. From scratch. Money no object."

He turned to me and shrugged helplessly.

"That's okay," I smiled, wanting to hurl that damn decorator off a cliff.

"This could take a while. Why don't you come to my place tonight, and we'll take up where we left off?"

I nodded, still numb with joy. But then I remembered.

"I can't. I've got my Seniors Class tonight."

"Then stop by after class."

He took me in his arms and kissed me again, our bodies touching in all the right places.

"To be continued," he whispered.

He let me out the back door of his shop, and I stumbled out into the alley, like a drunk on a bender. There was only one thing I knew for certain:

I was definitely going to have to shave my legs.

* * *

I made my way back to my Corolla, wondering if it was humanly possible to lose fifteen pounds in eight hours. (What this country needs is a chain of Same-Day Liposuction Centers.) Unable to come up with a miracle weight-loss plan, I decided to buy myself a new bra and panties. If my body couldn't be fab, at least my underwear would.

I drove over to Bloomingdale's in Century City and headed upstairs to the lingerie department. I waded through racks of panties that seemed to come in three sizes: Tiny, Tinier, and I've-Seen-More-Cotton-on-the-Top-of-an-Aspirin-Bottle.

Finally, hidden in a corner, I found the Realistic Sizes and picked up a sexy black-lace bra-and-panty set. I tried them on in the dressing room, hoping there were no jaded security guards watching me on a hidden camera and sniggering at my cellulite. I surveyed myself in the three-way mirror. If I sucked in my gut and squinted my eyes, I actually looked pretty good.

Given the fact that I had absolutely no new business coming in, I couldn't afford to buy anything else. Which is why I immediately stopped off at Ann Taylor and bought myself a new blazer and silk blouse. And then, feeling guilty about having spent so much, I economized by *not* buying a $250 pair of shoes at Joan & David, and buying a $60 bottle of citrusy Calvin Klein cologne instead.

Telling myself this crazy spending spree simply had to stop, I drove over to a hair salon in Brentwood and got an $80 haircut, a $20 pedicure, and a $30 parking ticket. (I forgot to put money in the meter.)

But it was worth it. I walked out of that salon with a headful of smooth, glossy Maria Shriver hair.

Finally I managed to make it home without spending any more money. Carefully wrapping my hair in a towel, I stepped in the shower and sudsed myself with a loofah till my skin was glowing. Then I shaved my legs, plucked my eyebrows, and waxed my bikini zone. It was a regular Exfoliation Festival. Unfortunately, there was nothing I could do about my cellulite except hope that Cameron liked to make love in the dark.

Yes, folks, I'd definitely decided to go to bed with the man. I'd had it with my monastic existence. Cameron had me tingling in places I didn't know could tingle, and I was ready to swing from some chandeliers.

I slipped into my new duds, spritzed myself in a cloud of my new cologne, and presented myself to Prozac for inspection.

"How do I look?" I asked, pirouetting. She gazed up from where she was napping on the sofa, and yawned. That's what I get for asking fashion advice from someone who has been known to walk around with dried pieces of you-know-what on her fanny.

I scooped her up in my arms and hugged her.

"Wish me luck, Pro."

She sniffed at my perfume and nuzzled her furry head under my chin.

"If I wind up loving him half as much as I love you," I whispered into her pink ear, "I'll be a mighty lucky lady."

Chapter Twenty-three

He looked me up and down and whistled. "Hubba, hubba," he said, lust in his eyes.

Unfortunately, the "he" in question wasn't Cameron, but Mr. Goldman. He grinned at me slyly as I walked into my Seniors Writing Class at the Shalom Retirement Home.

"Got a hot date tonight?"

It was all I could do to keep from leaping on the table and shouting, "Yes! Yes! Yes! With a man who turns my thighs to Jell-O!"

Instead I managed to smile demurely and say: "As a matter of fact, Mr. Goldman, I do happen to have a date tonight."

"With the gay guy?"

"He's not gay," I muttered through clenched teeth.

"Yeah. Right. Just like Liberace wasn't gay."

Mrs. Pechter shook her head in annoyance. "Don't mind him, Ms. Austen. Everyone knows he's impossible." Then she turned to Mr. Goldman and hissed, "Put a sock in it, Abe."

My sentiments, exactly.

"You look pretty as a picture," she said, turning back to me. The other ladies cooed in agreement.

I blushed as I took my seat at the head of the table.

"Okay, who wants to read first?"

Down at the end of the table, Mrs. Vincenzo raised her hand.

"You're on, Mrs. V."

Bette Vincenzo stood up, as she always did to read her essay, holding her slim body erect, her long hair flowing loose down her back.

"'My Fourth Husband,' by Bette Vincenzo," she began.

I didn't hear a single syllable of Mrs. Vincenzo's fourth attempt at matrimony. Try as I might to pay attention, my thoughts kept drifting back to Cameron. Mr. Goldman was wrong, wrong, wrong. Cameron wasn't gay. I'd felt hard evidence to the contrary rolling around with him on the antique sleigh bed. He liked women, that was for sure. And miraculously enough, he liked me! I still couldn't get over it. Cameron Bannick, he of the crinkly blue eyes and lissome body, actually liked me, Jaine Austen, she of the wiry brown hair and generous thighs.

I saw Mrs. Vincenzo's lips moving, but the words coming out of her mouth faded into the background, like Muzak in an elevator. I got out my looseleaf binder and turned to an empty page. I picked up my pen and started writing, as if making notes on her essay.

But I wasn't making notes. I was regressing shamelessly back to my high school days, covering the page with doodles. *Cameron & Jaine. Mrs. Cameron Bannick. J.A. loves C.B.* Any minute now, I expected to hear my old high school principal's voice on a P.A. system, announcing that tickets were still available for the spring prom.

I drew valentines and daisies and kittens with big eyes. At one point, I looked up and saw Mr. Goldman giving me a fishy stare, as if he knew exactly what I was doing. But I ignored him and kept on doodling until I filled the page. I gazed at my handiwork proudly, thinking that one of these days I really should enroll in an art class.

I doodled my way through Mrs. Ratner's grand-children and Mrs. Pechter's trip to Israel. I'd filled two pages with my lovestruck scribbles, and turned the page to start on a fresh piece of paper when I saw it: a parking ticket. Wedged between two pages.

At first I thought it was the parking ticket I'd gotten that afternoon in Brentwood. But then I saw that it wasn't issued to a Corolla, but to a Jeep. Cameron's Jeep. I recognized the license plate number.

I remembered the night Cameron came to class with me and drove me home in his Jeep, the night I bent over and picked up my looseleaf from his messy backseat, ashamed of my ample tush. Little did I realize that far from being turned off by my derriere, Cameron had actually lusted after it.

In the process of gathering my scattered papers, I must've shoved the parking ticket inside my looseleaf by mistake. I'd have to give it to Cameron right away. The deadline for paying the ticket had probably come and gone. I checked to see the date the ticket had been written. February Fourteenth. Valentine's Day. But that couldn't be. That was the night of Stacy's murder. Cameron was in San Francisco then. And this ticket was issued in Los Angeles. In Westwood. On Bentley Avenue.

The scene of the crime.

It didn't make sense. Had Cameron been in town that night? Was he somehow involved in Stacy's murder?

Impossible, I told myself. The owner of the bed & breakfast in San Francisco said he'd been at her restaurant the night of the murder. Was it possible that she was covering up to protect Cameron? Now that I thought about it, I had no actual proof that he was with her that night.

Suddenly I felt queasy. Had Cameron lied about Stacy? He said he hardly knew her. But maybe he'd known her very well. Maybe he'd been having an affair with her, like every other man in the Western Hemisphere. But even if he had, why would he want to kill her? He wasn't the type to blow up in a jealous rage like Devon. And unlike Daryush or Andy, he had no wealthy wife that Stacy could use as leverage in a blackmail plot.

I slammed my looseleaf shut, disgusted with myself. What was wrong with me? Here I'd finally met a wonderful guy, and I was accusing him of murder! I was sabotaging the relationship before it even started. I knew perfectly well that Cameron hadn't been having an affair with Stacy. She wasn't his type. The only woman he'd been "involved" with in Bentley Gardens was Marian Hamilton.

I knew what was going on. I was probably so afraid of getting close to someone, after my disastrous marriage to The Blob, that I was manufacturing reasons to scurry back to my safe cocoon of celibacy. I was afraid of getting laid, that was what this was all about. First thing tomorrow, I decided, I was going to make an appointment with a shrink.

I tried to concentrate on Mrs. Pechter's adventures at the Wailing Wall, but it was no use. I couldn't forget that damn parking ticket. I could give myself all the psychobabble lectures in the world, but I still had a horrible feeling in the pit of my stomach that Cameron was somehow involved with Stacy's murder.

I sat through the rest of the class in a daze, counting the minutes till nine o'clock. Mr. Goldman had just started reading the latest installment in "My Life as a Carpet Salesman" when I cut him short.

"I'm sorry, but that's all we have time for tonight." With trembling hands I gathered my things and headed for the door.

"Have a nice time on your date!" Mrs. Pechter called out. The other ladies echoed her sentiments, telling me how pretty I looked and to "enjoy yourself, dollink."

"I still say he's gay," Mr. Goldman muttered.

I waved good-bye, forcing my lips into a smile, and headed for the ladies' room. I needed desperately to splash some cold water on my face.

I walked into the dimly lit bathroom at the end of the corridor and was surprised to see a young woman, her back toward me, brushing her hair. What was a young girl doing at the Shalom Retirement Home?

But then she turned around and I saw that it wasn't a young woman, after all, but Mrs. Vincenzo. With her long hair and slim body, I'd mistaken her for someone much younger. And suddenly I was reminded of Marian Hamilton and her long blond hair. How easy it would have been, in the right lighting, to mistake her for a young woman. A young woman like Stacy. Hadn't Cameron told me how much the two of them looked alike? I could easily picture someone walking into a dimly lit bedroom and mistaking Marian for Stacy.

Or mistaking Stacy for Marian.

Mrs. Vincenzo finished brushing her hair and grinned.

"Have fun tonight, honey," she said, and headed out the door.

I clutched the sink for support. Waves of nausea were churning at the back of my throat.

A horrible scenario had begun to spin itself out in my mind.

What if Cameron was the killer? But what if he'd killed the wrong person? What if it was Marian he'd meant to kill, and not Stacy? After all, he'd been away in San Francisco for a month. He'd have no way of knowing that Marian had already died and that Stacy had moved into her apartment.

So he comes down to Los Angeles and parks his Jeep down the street so that no one in the building will realize he's there. Then he lets himself into Marian's apartment, with a key she'd no doubt given him.

The living room is dark, and he doesn't notice the furniture's changed. Besides, he's not thinking about furniture. He's got more important things on his mind. Quietly, he slips down the corridor to the bedroom. There he sees Stacy asleep, her back toward him, her blond hair splayed out on her pillow. In the dark, her hair looks just like Marian's. He sees the ThighMaster on the floor. The perfect murder weapon. He naturally assumes it's Marian's. She was proud of her body and liked to work out. So he picks up the bulky piece of metal and bludgeons Stacy to death—only to discover when he's done that he's killed the wrong woman.

But why? Why would Cameron have killed Marian? He seemed genuinely fond of her.

I had no idea why the man of my dreams would have beaten the life out of a faded starlet.

But he did. Of that, I was certain.

Which is why I spent the next fifteen minutes bent over a toilet bowl at the Shalom Retirement Home, puking my guts out.

Eventually I managed to pry myself away from the toilet bowl and drive back to my apartment.

No way was I going to keep my date with Cameron. I'd call him and tell him I wasn't feeling well—which was no lie. My stomach was growling, and my head was pounding. As soon as I got home, I collapsed on the sofa with a package of frozen peas on my forehead and Prozac on my belly.

Don't ask me how I knew with such utter certainty that Cameron was the killer. I just did. I'd been an idiot to fall for him. I should have known he wasn't really interested in me. There is an unwritten rule of mating, as far as I'm concerned: Beautiful People want Beautiful People. They rarely wind up with Commoners. Mel Gibson does not date Kathy Bates.

I could see now that Cameron had been dating me to keep tabs on me. Once he realized I was investigating the murder, he wanted to make sure I didn't discover the truth.

Yes, I was convinced Cameron was a killer. What I couldn't figure out was why?

What possible reason could Cameron have for wanting to kill Marian? A crime of passion? Hardly. And it couldn't have been money. She didn't leave him anything in her will, except for that framed photo of herself. Not exactly a windfall. The picture was probably worth six bucks, maximum, to a Hollywood trivia collector.

The phone rang. Too exhausted to move, I let the machine get it.

"Hi, Jaine. It's me." His voice sounded boyish. Innocent. "Just calling to see where you were. I thought you'd be here by now. Oh, well. I guess you're on your way."

Fat chance.

I stayed right where I was on the sofa, stroking Prozac and staring at the ceiling. After a while, my frozen peas started melting. I reached over to put them on the coffee table and grabbed a magazine to use as a coaster.

And that's when everything started to make sense.

Because the magazine I grabbed wasn't a magazine, but the catalogue from Christie's auction house.

Suddenly I remembered the picture of Cary Grant. The one that sold for $123,000. Something about it had looked familiar at the time. And now I knew what it was: the frame. *It was the frame that Marian had left Cameron in her will.*

Flinging the peas on the carpet, I started rifling through the pages of the catalogue until I found the photo of Cary Grant. Sure enough, it was in the same frame that had held Marian's picture.

Another scenario began forming in my mind:

A has-been actress owns a very valuable frame. Maybe it was given to her by a wealthy lover. She probably doesn't even realize how much it's worth. But then she meets a charming young antiques dealer who takes one look at the frame and knows it's a gold mine. He doesn't tell her, of course.

Instead, he befriends her and gets her to leave it to him in her will, as a sentimental memento.

Maybe at first he's not even thinking of murder. But then things get tough for him financially. His antiques shop is having a dry spell. And he needs cash badly. So he devises a plot to kill her, only he winds up killing the wrong blonde.

It all made perfect sense. Just that very afternoon, hadn't Cameron told me how he'd come into money, as a result of a big "sale"?

I reached for the phone and put in a call to Detective Rea. He was gone for the day, but I told the sergeant on duty to track him down and have him call me back as soon as possible.

I hung up, my nerves totally shot. I looked around my apartment and suddenly I knew I didn't want to spend the night there, alone, with nothing for protection but a cat with a compulsive eating problem. So I called Kandi, and asked if I could spend the night at her place. She said sure, fine, and asked if I'd mind picking up some Häagen-Dazs French Vanilla on my way over.

I hung up and started throwing things into my gym bag. I hadn't gotten very far when the phone rang. I leapt at it eagerly.

"Detective Rea?"

"No. It's Cameron."

Oh, God. I'd blundered. Badly.

"Hi, Cameron." I strained to keep the fear out of my voice. "I was expecting a call from Detective Rea. I wanted to talk to him about Daryush. I really think he's our killer."

"Can't you forget about the murder for one night?" he sighed. "I thought you were coming over for some hugging and munching."

He sounded sweet. Sexy. Utterly innocent. So

why were the hairs on the back of my neck standing on end?

"Cameron, I can't. I'm feeling terrible. Must have been something I ate. I've been throwing up all night."

"Let me come to your place and take care of you."

"No!" I shouted. "I mean, no . . . I'll be fine. Really."

"You sure?"

"I'm sure."

"Make yourself some chicken soup."

"I will."

"I miss you."

"Me too," I managed to choke out. "But I better go now. I think I'm going to be sick again." Which wasn't far from the truth.

I hung up, bathed in sweat. I only hoped he believed my cock-and-bull story about Daryush. More than ever, I wanted to get out of my apartment. I threw some pajamas into my gym bag, along with a toothbrush and an ancient bottle of Valium left over from my divorce.

I grabbed my car keys and was heading for the front door when I stopped in my tracks. I'd forgotten all about Prozac. I couldn't leave her alone in the apartment. I didn't know exactly what it was I was afraid of, but I *did* know that I'd never forgive myself if anything happened to her.

So I grabbed her cat carrier from the hall closet. Which was, of course, a fatal mistake. The minute she saw it, she undoubtedly thought, "Uh-oh, another trip to that irritating veterinarian who keeps sticking thermometers up my butt."

The next thing I knew, she was stubbornly entrenched under the sofa, just beyond my reach.

"C'mon, Prozac, honey, I swear we're not going to the vet's. We're going to Auntie Kandi's and I'll let you eat Häagen-Dazs French Vanilla till your tummy is as big as a cantaloupe. I promise."

But she wouldn't budge. I pleaded, I cooed, I threatened. Finally, I got smart and opened a can of gourmet liver innards. I held it out to her and crooned, "Mmmmmm, yummy liver. Mmmmmm, good."

A pink nose emerged from under the sofa. A large tummy soon followed. I snatched my beloved furball and tossed her into the carrier, along with the liver.

"I swear," I said, as she glared at me from her tiny prison, "we're not going to the vet's."

Then I grabbed my gym bag and opened the front door.

Only to find Cameron standing there. With a can of chicken noodle soup in one hand. And a gun in the other.

Chapter
Twenty-four

"I didn't really think you were sick," Cameron said, pushing me back into my apartment with the butt of his gun, "but I brought some soup anyway."

He smiled his crinkly-eyed grin and shoved me down onto the sofa. Prozac hissed from her carrier, clawing at the latch.

"Hush now, kitty." He took the carrier from my hands and hurled it across the room, Prozac howling in protest.

"So," he said, dropping the can of soup onto the coffee table. "You figured everything out, didn't you?"

I nodded numbly.

"What a comedy of errors, huh?"

"I wouldn't exactly call it a comedy."

He slouched down comfortably into my over-stuffed armchair and aimed his gun at my left breast.

"I go to kill Marian, but I have no idea that she's already dead and buried. So I wind up offing that stupid bimbo by mistake. Can you believe my rotten luck?"

"Stacy's luck wasn't too hot, either."

"Oh, come on. She was a piece of trash. No great loss to humanity."

Now he aimed the gun at my right breast.

"So how did you guess it was me? I had an airtight alibi. I was in San Francisco the night of the murder, having dinner at the Union Street Inn. The proprietor of the inn, one Ann Garrity, will swear to that."

"Is she your girlfriend? Is that how you got her to lie for you?"

"That cow? My girlfriend? Please, I practically threw up when I had to sleep with her. I just closed my eyes and thought of Sharon Stone."

"Is that what you were going to do with me tonight? Think of Sharon Stone?"

He grinned apologetically. Like a kid with his hand caught in the cookie jar.

"Maybe just a little."

A fresh wave of nausea washed over me. I would've puked, but I had nothing left to throw up. So I just sat there, listening to the sounds of my gut heaving and Prozac scratching at her cage.

Cameron looked down at the coffee table and saw the Christie's auction catalogue.

"So that's how you figured it out. You were there. At the auction."

I nodded. "I knew something about the picture was familiar, and tonight I finally figured out what it was. The frame."

"It's a beauty, isn't it?"

"Yes, but where did you get the picture of Cary Grant?"

"Oh, that. Marian actually dated him for a while.

He gave her a framed photo of himself. Then he dumped her for someone else. Barbara Hutton or Randolph Scott, I forget who. Anyhow, she got pissed and covered his picture with that cheesy starlet snapshot of herself. The first time I saw it, I knew the frame was worth a lot of money. And the picture of Cary Grant just made it more valuable."

"So you became Marian's new best friend."

"Right again, Sherlock." Cameron was playing with the gun now, twirling it like a cowboy in a bad Western.

"She gave you the key to her apartment, just in case of an emergency, never dreaming that the emergency would be you bashing her head in."

"Hey, I never wanted to kill Marian. She was a harmless old bat. The person I really wanted to kill was my stockbroker. He got me into some very stupid investments. Otherwise I wouldn't have dreamed of knocking her off."

"And the key you gave Daryush the day he caught us breaking into Stacy's apartment. It really *was* the key to the apartment. That's how you let yourself in the night of the murder."

"That idiot Daryush. If he'd only changed the locks after Marian died, Stacy would be alive today. Not that it matters. Like I said, she's no great loss."

With that, he picked up a magazine from the coffee table and hurled it at the cat carrier, where Prozac was moaning piteously. I wanted to leap up and strangle him, but figured that wasn't exactly a smart way to go, not with his gun aimed straight at my chest.

"And after the murder, you hid out in your own apartment. Which is why none of the tenants saw or heard anyone running away."

"Yep. I was lying in bed watching *Jeopardy* when

Howard showed up for his date. Poor shmuck." He shook his head pityingly. "Anyhow, I had a restful night's sleep, and then the next morning at dawn I snuck out to my Jeep and drove to the beach for a few hours. Then I came back just in time to meet you."

He looked at me with what I could swear was genuine fondness and clicked something on the gun.

"The safety catch," he explained. "It's off now." He sighed wearily. "I'm going to have to kill you, of course. And it's really a shame. Because I like you." He actually managed to look sad.

"Well, don't do it if it's going to make you unhappy."

He smiled again, that wonderful grin that could soften cement.

"That's what I like about you. You make me laugh. Too bad you couldn't have minded your own business."

"I think I should tell you," I said, trying to keep the hysteria out of my voice, "I just spoke with Detective Rea and told him that you killed Stacy."

Cameron said nothing. Just sat there looking at me, trying to figure out if I was bluffing. He figured right.

"Nice try," he said finally. "But I don't believe you."

"I did. I swear. If you kill me, he'll know it's you."

"I'll take my chances. Every day you suspect someone new. I doubt the cops take you very seriously. I'm hoping they'll pin your murder on Andy. They'll probably think he had you killed to keep you from testifying at his trial."

"They'll never believe that."

"Really? It works for me."

He aimed the gun straight at my heart.

"Sorry, hon. I don't have a choice."

Just as he was about to pull the trigger, an angry ball of fur burst out of her cage and came hurtling across the room. Prozac, that incredible animal, had clawed the latch free.

I'm sure you've read stories of heroic cats who rescued their owners-in-distress by attacking intruders or dialing 911 with their paws.

Prozac isn't one of them.

She whizzed past Cameron and scooted under the sofa, scared out of her wits. But the sudden movement threw him off guard. I grabbed the can of chicken noodle soup from the coffee table, and hurled it at him, knocking the gun from his hand.

The gun went skittering across the room. Cameron and I went skittering after it. The good news is, I reached it first. The bad news is, Cameron grabbed it out of my hands before I could even find the trigger. And then, just as he was taking aim at my chest for the fifth time that evening, we heard footsteps clomping up the path. A bunch of cops came bursting through the front door, guns drawn.

"Okay, Cameron," Detective Rea shouted, "drop it."

And he did.

Epilogue

Remind me never to badmouth Lance again. It turns out that darling man and thoughtful neighbor had his ear glued to my wall, as usual, and as soon as he realized I was in trouble, he called the police. If it hadn't been for him, at this very moment I'd be plot mates with Stacy Lawrence at The Vale of Peace.

As a gesture of gratitude, I took him to dinner at a local trattoria where we spent a good part of the evening listening to the couple in the next booth breaking up. This eavesdropping thing can be quite addicting, once you get the hang of it.

Anyhow, Lance isn't nearly as bad as I thought. He actually likes his job selling shoes at Neiman Marcus, and has a whole repertoire of shoe salesman jokes. Like the one about the bimbo customer who asks, "What have you got to go with a short, fat millionaire?" (I never said they were funny.)

After a few glasses of chianti, Lance said he could

get me an employee discount on Neiman Marcus shoes. So instead of a quatrillion dollars for a pair of Manolo Blahniks, I'd only be paying half a quatrillion. But it was sweet of him to offer.

Naturally, they arrested Cameron and charged him with all sorts of unpleasant things. Like murder, attempted murder, and assault with a deadly ThighMaster.

And believe it or not, Detective Rea was kind enough to give me credit for solving the case. Ever since he saved my life, he's been surprisingly sweet. He actually apologized for not having taken me seriously, and he's called me several times just to make sure I'm okay.

Anyhow, he sang my praises to the news media, and they ran a story about me in the *Los Angeles Times*. With my picture and everything. True, it was right next to an ad for vericose vein removal. But lots of people read it.

The story mentioned that I was a freelance writer, and my phone has been ringing off the hook with job offers. In fact, just yesterday I was asked to write a brochure for a national plumbing corporation. (I'm not at liberty to divulge their name; let's just say it rhymes with Toto Tooter.) So I guess you could say I'm back in the toilet again.

I have to confess I miss being a detective. Yes, I know it was dangerous. And I know I almost got mowed down by a BMW. And gunned down by a psychopath. But it was exciting. My blood was rushing, my corpuscles were puscling.

Which is why I've signed up for a course at the Learning Annex. *How To Be a Private Eye.* Kandi's coming with me. Not to meet men. I'm happy to say she's stuck by her resolution to give up the whole manhunting thing. No, she's coming to get story ideas for a new show she's working on, a spin-off of *Beanie & The Cockroach* called *Maggot, P.I.*

Who knows? I just might wind up making a career change and become a detective. One of the growing breed of PI's with PMS.

In fact, I've already been working on an idea for an ad in the Yellow Pages. What do you think?

Jaine Austen, Discreet Inquiries
Work Done with Pride, not Prejudice

I know. It needs work.

As for men, my encounter with Cameron has set me back light-years in the Meaningful Relationship department. After The Blob, I thought I'd never love again. After Cameron, I know I never will. It's over, as far as men are concerned. I'm happy to live out my life single, one of those crazy old ladies whose Significant Other is her cat.

So that about wraps it up. Things have pretty much gone back to normal. Mr. Goldman is still irritating the kapok out of everyone at the Shalom Retirement Home. Andy Bruckner is still doing lunch at Spago—and doing Jasmine in the back-seat of his BMW. Prozac is still eating like a long-shoreman. And the last I heard, Howard was dating a waitress at the House of Wonton.

Oh, wait a minute. There's the phone. I'll be right back.

You'll never guess who that was. Detective Rea. How's this for crazy? He wanted to know if I was free for dinner tonight.

He's got to be kidding, right? Me, go out with a person of the masculine persuasion? After what I've just been through? Ridiculous. Impossible. Out of the question.

He's picking me up at eight.

Please turn the page for

an exciting sneak peek of

Laura Levine's

next Jaine Austen mystery

LAST WRITES

coming in hardcover in July 2003!

Chapter One

I should've known there was trouble ahead when I saw the sign over the studio gate:
MIRACLE STUDIOS
"If It's a Good Picture, It's a Miracle"
Miracle Studios, for those of you lucky enough never to have been there, is a sorry collection of soundstages in the scuzziest section of Hollywood, a part of town where the hookers outnumber the parking meters two to one.

But when I drove onto the Miracle lot that hazy Monday morning, I was a happy camper. I, Jaine Austen, was about to become a bona fide Hollywood Sitcom Writer. After years of toiling at my computer as a freelance writer, churning out brochures and resumes and personals ads, I was about to strike it rich in show biz. No longer would I have to come up with fictional resumes for college grads with room-temperature IQs. Or slogans for my biggest client, Toiletmasters Plumbers (*In a Rush to Flush? Call Toiletmasters*).

I owed my good fortune to my best friend, Kandi

Tobolowski. Six weeks earlier, she'd called me with the news:

"Guess what," she said. "I've kissed the cockroach good-bye!"

The cockroach to whom she was referring was the star insect of a Saturday morning cartoon show, *Beanie & The Cockroach*, a heartwarming saga of a chef named Beanie and his pet cockroach, Fred. Kandi had been a staff writer on *Beanie* for more years than she cared to admit. Like most animation writers, she'd long dreamed of landing a job in the far more prestigious world of live-action television.

And that day had finally arrived. Her agent had taken enough time off from lunch at Spago to line up a job for her on a comedy called *Muffy 'n Me*— a Saturday morning syndicated show about a buxom teenage girl who gets hit on the head with a volleyball and develops magical powers.

As the Miracle bigwigs pitched it to the network, "It's *Bewitched* with tits."

Okay, so it wasn't going to win any Emmys. But it was a big step up from the cockroach, and Kandi was thrilled. So was I, two weeks later, when she told me she'd managed to get me a script assignment on the show.

At first, I was terrified. After all, I wasn't much of a comedy writer. But then *Muffy 'n Me* wasn't much of a comedy. So, after chaining myself to my computer, armed with only my wits and a copy of Henny Youngman's *Giant Book of One-Liners*, I managed to complete my comedic masterpiece, "Cinderella Muffy." It's all about what happens when Muffy magically changes her ratty bathrobe into a glam prom dress, only to have the spell wear off in the middle of the prom, leaving her stranded on the dance floor, doing the Funky Chicken in her jammies.

I know, it sounds ghastly to someone of your refined tastes. But remember, we're talking Hollywood here, the town that brought you *My Mother the Car* and *The Gong Show*. The head writers loved it! Okay, so maybe they didn't love it. But they liked it. Enough to invite me to be a "guest writer" on the show for a week. And here's the truly wonderful part. If they liked working with me, they were going to offer me a staff job! And if I did well on *Muffy*, it would be only a matter of time before I made the leap from syndication to prime time. Do you know how much prime-time sitcom writers make? Well, neither do I. But I hear it's scads. Truckloads of really big bucks. Think Bill Gates. Think Donald Trump. Think plumbers on overtime!

Ever since I'd handed in my script, I'd had visions of Seinfeldian contracts dancing in my head. I'd already mentally bought my beach house in Malibu, complete with his and hers Jaguars for me and my husband. Not that I had a husband, but I was sure I'd pick one up along the way.

All of which explains why I was in a jolly mood that morning as I drove past the wino sunning himself at the studio gates and onto the Miracle lot. I pulled up in front of the guard booth, where an ancient man with rheumy eyes and the unlikely name of Skippy asked me where I was headed.

"*Muffy 'n Me!*" I grinned.

Was it my imagination or did I see a trace of pity in those rheumy old eyes?

"Park over there," he said, waving to a tiny spot next to the commissary dumpster.

I parked my trusty Corolla in the shadow of the

dumpster and stepped out onto the lot, trying to ignore the smell of rotting garbage. Swinging my brand-new attaché case, I headed over to the office I was to share with Kandi, eager to start on this exciting new chapter of my life. Somehow it still didn't seem real. I had to keep reminding myself that I actually had a job at Miracle Studios.

Of course, I didn't know it at the time, but the real miracle was that I'd live to tell about it.